A WYATT
BOOK *for*

W

— ST. —
MARTIN'S
PRESS

RIDER

MARIAN
FRANCES
WOLBERS

A WYATT BOOK *for* ST. MARTIN'S PRESS
NEW YORK

RIDER. Copyright © 1996 by Marian Frances Wolbers. All rights reserved. Printed in the United States of America. No part of this book may be used or reproduced in any manner whatsoever without written permission except in the case of brief quotations embodied in critical articles or reviews. For information, address A Wyatt Book for St. Martin's Press, 175 Fifth Avenue, New York, N.Y. 10010.

Illustrations by Barbara Fritz

Design by Ellen R. Sasahara

Library of Congress Cataloging-in-Publication Data

Wolbers, Marian.
    Rider / Marian Frances Wolbers.—1st ed.
      p.   cm.
    "A Wyatt book for St. Martin's Press."
    ISBN 0-312-14718-X
    I. Title
    PS3573.O456R53   1996
    813'.54—dc20   96-3119
                                         CIP

First Edition: November 1996

10 9 8 7 6 5 4 3 2 1

To Kimie

For spiritual guidance, I am grateful to Linda Barnett for showing me how to open myself to hear Mai's story. I give thanks also to my whole family, and to my friends Yuko Kashiwagi, Ruth Sloane, and JoAnn Jones for their sincere and caring support. For unbridled encouragement from the very beginning, I thank Ken Bloom and Joel Bleifuss. For believing in me, my heartfelt thanks go to Stuart Grunther.

For inspiration, and the special kind of supportive shoulder that only a fellow writer can lend, I am grateful to my dear friend, novelist Lillian Rodberg.

For unwavering conviction regarding the tale of *Rider,* I bow my head to my agent, Frances Collin. Barbara Fritz provided artwork that captured what I saw in my mind's eye, while Iris Bass looked over the entire manuscript as only a visionary editor can, with a clear eye and an unparalleled literary sensitivity.

Finally, there's the matter of Joe Champagne—who provided the space and quiet I needed to complete this book, giving me unconditional, generous shares of his faith, laughter, and artistic understanding at a critical time in my life. Thanks, Joe.

CONTENTS

RIDER

1 THE TRUTH ABOUT CHRISTMAS AND WOMEN LYING ACROSS THE SEATS

To my American half sisters, with love. Mai Asahikawa

I have been riding the trains now for over a year. Not every day, though it might appear that way, and not continuously even when I do spend the day riding. Often I take breaks on the plastic benches along the platform. The seats are very much like those you find in airports and bus stations, sort of rounded to hold only one ass at a time, and never comfortable unless you are prepared to sit for a long time. There are some men who sleep on them stretched out full length, their bodies held up at key points by the ridged edges; these men look very comfortable. I have never seen a woman lying across the seats.

From the benches you can feel the trains coming in before you see the lights. You can watch the conductors, let as many trains in and out as you care to, and get on again. In fact, the plastic seats are a real pleasure. Not only are they in the thick of detraining passengers, but they are crowded by future riders before the trains come.

Today I took a seat break close to noon. There was a smoke fire in the ashtray at the end of the bench—a rather bad fire, I was thinking—so I rose and picked up the plastic bottle attached to the pillar: it held water and hung to the side of the ashtray by a white string. I took aim, squeezed the bottle, and when the fire seemed to be out, I sat back down on the orange seat, waited for the next train to come in.

The red train rolled in, a noisy one with a grating squeal of the brakes. Steel on steel. The people on either side of me rose quickly and crowded round the spot where they figured the doors would open, leaving a scraggly parting in between themselves so that passengers exiting the train would have a place to go.

And then an astounding thing happened. Here it was, high noon—a peak in the day, of course—but absolutely not a single person got out of the train at that door when it opened right in front of me. What's more, the parting that had been created for anyone exiting remained and defined itself still more clearly so that a whole person could have walked neatly between the people who were lined up to get on—there really was that much space in there. This incredible opening actually paused for a moment before it dissolved into people's backs.

Ah, soon it will be Christmas, I said to myself. That's what it is. *Gokigen desu* (The moods are good). When the next red train screeched its way in, I stood on the left side of the door along with a smartly dressed suede matron and several gray suits. No seats at noon; I positioned myself in the middle of the car and looked around. A pair of bundled-up kids stood in front of me. Boots, but no gloves. As the train gained momentum, it jerked suddenly and all of us standing at the center lurched forward, knocked into each other, and fell on the group in the area between the doors. Then the train smoothed out and everyone regained balance and reestablished space.

It was warm in the train. I was comfortably squeezed between two businessmen reading comic books. In the seats, everyone looked asleep. All was well. Only the ads were different from yesterday. They must have been changed in the morning. Van Gogh was in town, the girls at the Hong King Palace were the hottest numbers in town, and, as I mentioned before, Christmas was in town.

Last year, Christmas was much the same. Degas was here, and

so were the same girls at the Hong Kong Palace. And last year and this year as every year, the magical season really started with slinky Christmas blondes like the one on a whiskey ad, and Asian snow bunnies on the slopes in Sapporo, and men holding beribboned skin conditioners—progressing until every sign in the subway was red and gold and glittery.

Last year sometime in the glitter period, I'd been riding the metropolitan lines quite a bit, and I went outside one evening to a little pork cutlet place in Bunkyo ward. It was convenient and I knew where it was. The girl who worked in the place had one single eyelid and one double. That is, one eyelid had a crease like a Caucasian eye, and the other had none, just smooth eyelid over eye. This combination that she had, I have been told, is considered very charming. Yes, charming is the word. Disconcerting, but charming. Though it was hardly the first time I had seen such a condition, this particular girl had a really startling pair of eyes, with unremarkable features in every other way—and she had very pretty eyes at that, so she was stared at by all the customers including myself; we just couldn't help it. The girl herself acted embarrassed about it, but she was very sweet, and once I became a regular, she relaxed a lot. Kimiko was her name. She couldn't have been more than eighteen.

"Hello." I came in and took the table closest to the door.

Kimiko was watching the television, which was high in a corner of the bar. She turned around when she heard me, and a slow smile grew and settled shyly on her face.

"It's been a while since you've dropped by." She filled a thick mug with tea and set it down on my table.

"Oh. Yes, well. You see, I've been all over town these past weeks. Going here, going there." It was true. I had been all over. Those days I was taking the metropolitan lines—not the private lines—across town and through town, and I even took a few trains that went above ground. Though it is not my habit now to take anything but the subway, at that time I had heard convincing rumors of earthquakes and I didn't want to be stuck in the subway when it happened. It may even have been that I was just taking the above-ground trains so I could sneak looks at the department store fronts that said MERRY CHRISTMAS and STARLIGHT CHRISTMAS, and there was a catchy one that went WISHING CHRISTMAS; also there was a sleigh ride on the top of Sono Department Store, up there on the roof. If you got out at Rokubashi at the front of the train going uptown, you could see signs for SUPER SLEIGH and actually hear the jingle bells and sounds of laughter. I seem to recall they were playing "Jingle Bells" over the loudspeakers, and probably another song, too.

"You're certainly busy," Kimiko said. "What will you have?"

The proprietor, Kimiko's father, looked up at that moment from a bleary-eyed group of men who were eating pork cutlets at the counter bar. He was taller than most men and wore his hair cropped like bristles, with a towel tied around his head. He had a broad, open face, and a buddy-buddy manner that kept his customers coming back for more, even though he wasn't particularly a good cook and somehow the cutlets had less meat than fat.

It so happened that this group of men were roaring with laughter and pouring each other beer and trying to pour beer for Kimiko's father, who was begging off, saying he had to cook for his customers at least another half hour, but in the meantime won't they all drink for him and he'd feel much better. This was what they were laughing at, and as they all raised glasses to perform their favors to their buddy, he happened to look my way and boomed out a hearty, "What'll it be?"

"Pork," I said. It was all they had anyway.

"One cutlet coming up!" boomed Kimiko's father. He smacked a breaded slice on the grill and turned back to the group of men with flushed faces. Kimiko had resumed looking at the TV.

"Anything on?" I asked.

"Yes, a Christmas show."

I watched it for a while. It was just like the train in a way, all red and gold and glittery. There was a woman singing a jazzed-up "White Christmas" ("I'm a' du-reamin' of a pa-pa-pa-pow! White Christmas . . . ") and she had on a furry white dress that was cut to her navel and her hair was all coiffeured with gold tinsel in it. My meal came just in time for a slew of commercials, two of which were the same ad repeated, and all of them pushing whiskey except for one—Swiss Alps chocolate with the taste of the mountains, which Rising Sun Candies has miraculously been able to manufacture right here in Tokyo. Somewhere during this I must have fallen asleep, for I awoke to find Kimiko's father sitting on the bar stool where his daughter had been, flipping the channels on the TV. The men who had been whooping it up were gone; so was Kimiko.

When he found his station, Kimiko's father turned around to laugh at me.

"Fell asleep, didn't you?" he said in his big voice. He turned back to the TV. It was the *Eleven O'Clock Hour,* a show for men. Tonight, the hosts were being quite emphatic that Christmas sex was for everybody, not just men, and that if you were a woman watching this show, just keep tuned, there's something in it for you (that was the male commentator speaking). The woman commentator nodded her approval, patted her hair, and smiled— "That's exactly right, Taroh"—whereupon Taroh led right into the first skit of the show.

A girl with long, beautiful, jet black hair goes to greet her husband at the door wearing nothing but a pair of lace panties with a reindeer embroidered across her bottom. She holds out her arms with her eyes closed, lips puckered for a kiss. Her husband looks happily surprised, then drops his briefcase, declaring, "Kissing is a bore!" and tackles her below the waist, whereupon she puts a surprised look on her face.

(End of Skit One.)

Next, there is a dancer who stands on a revolving stage about a meter in circumference. She is sending off light beams from shiny jewelry that adorns her neck. She wears a blond Afro wig. Her eyelashes hit her brows and rosy circles gleam on her cheeks.

She moves her hips sensually and rubs her hands up and down her blue jeans. Her breasts are free-swinging and large but not firm. The music is some type of disco soul.

Back to the skits, and this time there's a lovely young woman sleeping soundly, a chimney at the foot of her bed. Down comes Santa Claus, a skinny little man with big glasses, boots first, carrying a big sack. He's singing a little ditty to himself: "Oh, Me-ri Ku-ri-su-masu . . . Oh, Me-ri Ku-ri-su-masu, da di da da da." He sees the girl in bed, rubs his hands together, and begins to remove his red trousers. She wakes to see him in his long johns and sits straight up in bed, breasts flying, arms stretched wide. "Oh, San-ta Ku-ra-su!" she exclaims, "I've waited a year for you!"

(End of Skit Two, and back to the dancer with the blond Afro, who is now wearing only a golden chastity belt and necklaces. She leads into three commercials.)

Then it's on to the next episode of "Oh, Merry Christmas." The same lovely young woman is in bed again and the chimney is in the same place. Santa comes down the chimney singing his little ditty and carrying his bag of goodies. She remains asleep. Skinny little Santa smiles lasciviously and takes out of the big red bag a sawed-off baseball bat. He grabs it and climbs under the covers. There is great commotion under the sheets. The girl wakes up to look into the camera with incredulous large eyes and exclaims, "My, San-ta Ku-ra-su! You're bigger than I thought!" She smiles and dives under the covers for more, ending the skit.

Back again to the dancer, who is looking rather tired, still dancing to the same disco soul, and then on to another commercial.

Suddenly I felt very tired. Kimiko's father hadn't moved. He wasn't laughing at the show, but he wasn't not laughing. He sat with his arms folded, one elbow leaning on the bar. I left then; not that I was afraid he was getting excited by the show, but because the trains would stop soon after twelve—although it crossed my mind that Kimiko's father might be just a touch horny, and that he was probably no more virtuous than anyone else. All things considered, it was time I moved on.

The street was gray and closed. It was snowing lightly. Wet flakes blew sideways around my head that night and all the way down the street. It seemed darker than usual. Was there no moon? A lock turned, clicked shut.

Suddenly, the moon slipped out from behind a cloud cover. It was a bright white half-moon, and I remember thinking, Well, there's that rabbit, that little guy up there pounding those rice cakes. *O-mochi*, they're called. For New Year's that's what for. Rice cakes for all the holiday rice-cake broilers—men, women, and children alike—who'll dip them in soy sauce thickened with sugar or wrap them in crispy seaweed. Rice cakes for all the soups that women make for New Year's morning. The rice cake gets gooey and long in the soup, carrots get snagged in the globby stuff, and—God! there is really nothing like that soup! What I wouldn't give to have some of that. I wouldn't make it for myself, though. Too much time, something missing in my recipe, I thought. Mama would be happy to see me on New Year's. She'd probably be very happy to see me then. And she makes very good soup.

Then I thought, if I were in America, I'd probably see the moon as the profile of a Caucasian man with a high nose. Or maybe Americans think of an American flag up there along with all the other things the astronauts left behind. Maybe Russians see a hammer and sickle. The Indians, a Gandhi spinning cotton. The Moors, a riderless horse rearing. The Greeks . . . what would the Greeks see? Athena perhaps. Or an olive tree. Shish kabob? It was all conceivable. If the country is different, is the vision different in that country regardless of nationality? That is, does the Swiss ambassador living in Tokyo see the rabbit or something else?

Once some while ago there was a newspaper article in something religious like the *Japan Christian* or *The Living God* or the *Japanese Christian Scientist*—one of those, anyway, something Mama had in the house. She wanted me to tell her who Eldridge Cleaver was, had I ever heard of him at college, or had the nuns ever talked about him in high school, and I told her yes, I'd heard of him, but it wasn't the nuns who told me, no way on earth did the nuns ever talk about Eldridge Cleaver. It was Mr. Dunning in the English Department at the university who assigned us *Soul on Ice* to read.

"Was it good?" she wanted to know. "Is it translated into Japanese?"

"Yes, it was good," I told her. "But are you sure you want to read it? I'll bet there's a translated version around, it's famous enough."

"What was it about?" she pressed. "Does it describe his revelations?"

I remember puzzling over that last question. Does it describe his revelations?

"Well, Mama," I said finally, "I suppose you could say he comes to some understanding about why he has raped women, though I never thought of it as a revelation exactly, just that he desires white women for the reasons that he and other black men do, America's oppression and all that, and . . . Mama? Mother! What are you doing there? Why are you praying?"

"Pray," she said.

"No, I'm not going to pray unless you tell me why."

At that, Mama opened her eyes long enough to hand me this article she had read in one of those religious magazines, just a short article describing Mr. Cleaver's religious experience in France of 1975 where he had this revelation and turned Christian. "Formerly Black Panther," was all it said; I am certain Mama must have thought "Black Panther" was a voodoo religion for American black heathens who do not yet know about Christ.

I read that article in partial shock. Eldridge Cleaver had a vision, it said. In the moon, while gazing at it one night, he saw first the face of himself, then the face of Castro, then Mao, and last, finally, the face of Christ, until all he could see was Christ, strong and gentle, an energetic and spiritual face. He fell on his knees and began to recite psalms. And I thought, Eldridge Cleaver? Raperof-women gun-packing revolutionary militant black leader of America? It was a profound shock, and I doubted the validity of the account. But there were other articles since then, little ones, and some talk among Americans I knew confirming it. Well, so after a while it wasn't hard to believe at all. It even made sense: he was, after all, an American, and the revelations he saw in the moon were men-in-the-moon. It was totally consistent with his cultural upbringing.

If Christ was the image of truth and enlightenment for Cleaver, was it because Cleaver was in France at the time? If he had been in Japan, mightn't he have seen the Buddha in the moon? If the Buddha was Truth, wouldn't that mean that Cleaver was full of delusions? And if Cleaver were right about Christ, then what of Nichiren and all the others who knew truth through the Buddha? Is truth cultural and has everything to do with images? Or are the images cultural, like the man-in-the-moon, and the truth is the same no matter what the image?

Suddenly I found myself deep in the subway and waiting for the next train already. When it came, there seemed to be something new about it—something that had always been there before, but so obvious that it could have been just that particular train. I waited for two trains to come in before deciding: It was true. Of the two front lights on an approaching subway train, the light closest to the wall—that is, the light farthest away from you—will appear closer than the other light on the platform side of the

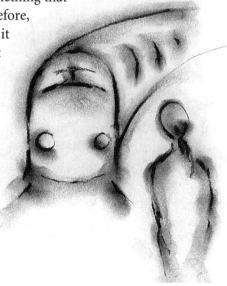

front car, which will seem to be a car or so behind the other light. Only when the train is quite close will the lights pull together and appear as they should look.

And this revelation came, I am sure, because I had been thinking about moons and round orbs of light.

All that was a year ago. Since that time I have come to trust a type of visual truth more than social ideas governing the trains, especially when it comes to women lying across the seats. But there is every possibility that there will be a woman lying there one day, her coat wrapped around her, her pocketbook a pillow. There's no reason why she won't be there with tousled black or brown or red hair and maybe boots on.

As a matter of fact, I used to think there were no station people, but when I began to see the same men picking at the same garbage bins in same stations every day, looking very unchanged from the night before, it seemed unlikely that they had been going to some nice little warm house to sleep at night. A station was, after all, one of the warmest places around. It had no wind, no rain, no cold, except for the few drafts that would chill any house, and there were plenty of opportunities for picking up reading material, half-smoked cigarettes, and also for having parties. It did seem that there were no women living in the stations.

But one day, about a year ago October, when the weather turned cold, there she was among a grand group of station people in Shinoka Station, the most famous subway haven in all of Tokyo. Gathered one hundred meters or so past the young glue sniffers, they were having a party, many of them sitting in a row, passing bottles. Some of the men were familiar; the one with the mustache and young look about him was new, and so was this woman, who was obviously female. Her hair was longish, tangled and matted, just like that of all the men except for the one who always wore a gray, shapeless hat and you really couldn't tell if he was bald or what. Her dark face was barely visible for the hair.

She wore ragged old baggy pants and a great black coat, and slung around her neck and shoulders were dark scarves and scraps of materials. She didn't look any different from the others in appearance or demeanor; she went through the garbage systematically and thoroughly, holding interesting articles up to inspect them and consider their value. From her manner and rapport with the group, it seemed certain that she was indeed a professional station person.

She caught my stare as I stood watching from the newsstand, a vantage point that kept me just out of sight of the men; her eyes were small and black and sharp. She scurried away just like every station person who catches a stare.

Fortunately, my eyes were very sharp that day, and I quickly drew a picture of her.

As I was drawing this, I thought: I should not have been surprised to see her, or stared so. Why could I not accept that she was a station person? I drew up the following list in my notebook, to explain to myself why women cannot do this sort of thing:

1. INVISIBILITY
Women tend to pass by station people, paint-thinner addicts, exposed men, crazy people talking to themselves, etc., without seeing them.

2. DANGERS (Physical)
Women cannot live a station existence. They might get raped by vagrant station men or passersby.

3. PRACTICAL DISADVANTAGE (Biological)
If they are premenopausal, how—not having money—can they supply themselves with sanitary napkins?

4. CULTURAL
Women just don't do things like become vagabond.
Women can get married and get their money from a man who works, and even if they don't have money (e.g., if they have a jobless and/or vagabond husband, etc.), SomeOne or SomeThing will take care of them so that they needn't live in the station. This is assuming that station people live in the station because they need to.

5. THE INNATE PERSONALITY OF WOMEN
Women don't want to be station people. Generally speaking, if they have no money or no place to go, they kill themselves quietly and in an acceptable manner.

Five ways to fool the mind into thinking untrue social thoughts.

2 | THE TRUTH ABOUT NOODLES

It was a good day for riding. Full of revelations. Loaded with encounters. Surrounded by people.

At Tokyo Station, half the lunch riders on the train got out, and I grabbed a nice seat next to the door so that I could lean my hand on the silver bar armrest and watch the other riders. Across the way sat a young woman with purple eyeshadow and a pink mouth. She held her purse on her lap with both hands and closed her eyes. Next to me was a college boy wearing loafers and studying English out loud.

" 'Give me a pound and a half of sugar, then, Tony. Oh, and a can of sweet corn, too, please.'

" 'Surely, Mrs. Martin. Anything else today?' "

The middle-aged woman sitting next to him was pretending to sleep, but periodically her eyelids would open slowly and she'd turn to look at the college boy in the grocery store, and then turn back to close her eyes once more.

" 'No, thank you, Tony. I think that's all.' "

Farther down, sitting immediately next to the middle-aged woman, were two old men dozing, both with their heads hanging forward; one was falling heavily forward as his shoulders slumped deeper and deeper into sleep, and the other was falling sideways onto the young *salary-man* (professional) next to him, who was himself taking a snooze with his head back and his arms folded across his chest. Front, side, and up the sleepers dozed. I sketched them quickly.

The standers in front of them had their eyes closed, too. They swayed blindly to the train's rhythm, and just as the train pulled into the next station, three standers and the salaryman woke up, looked around, and lined up quickly at the door.

"Nohara! Nohara Station!" sang the conductor.

" 'That's a long list you have there, Mrs. Martin.' "

"Change here for the Chiyoda, Tozai, and—"

" 'Yes, we had guests for the weekend and they ate us out of—' "

"—leave anything behind."

" '—house and home. Out of house and home. I'm out of everything today, Tony.' "

"The doors are going to close. They're closing!" sang the conductor.

Shsh-thwump.

New riders had slid into the vacant seats and already had their eyes closed. The middle-aged woman two seats away was fully awake now, and for a brief moment our eyes met in the window opposite, just passing, then off to the side, and then back to the window. The college boy was mouthing sounds, but no words came out. The train was very quiet.

Two women in employee uniforms stood in identical low black pumps near the door. Both had fresh lipstick drawn neatly on their mouths. The girl with full lips said something in a deep tone to her friend, who gave one short nod in answer, and then the friend said something else in the same deep tone and her friend nodded again. This went on for some stops. Talk, talk, talk, nod. Talk, talk, talk, nod.

Both women looked out the window. They focused straight ahead, and then let their eyes follow the scenery for a time, their pupils traveling to the far corner of their eye sockets, whereupon they returned their eyes to center, and the whole process repeated. Follow more outer-train scenery, hang on to it, return to center, follow again.

This kind of viewing causes a loss of scenery in between, something that is perhaps unfortunate on an above-ground train, but in the subway the loss is not so terribly crucial as there are only stretches of concrete wall with stations in between to focus on. Actually, it is rather a good way of viewing, I thought, as it allows the viewers to focus for a longer time on one scene.

The loss in the middle bothered me at one time, but I grew used to it, thinking that, well, peripherally all scenes are there anyway and so not completely lost. Besides, if I closed my eyes for a nap, I missed it all forever.

But of all the ways to kill eye time, that sort of thing is not really suited for the subway, except as a sort of exercise. Most riders prefer looking in the direction of the opposite window, remaining without focus, hanging their vision somewhere out in space above the opposite person's head or in suspension midway between the seats. From either of these vantage points, the possibility for direct or indirect glancing at other riders is right there.

And all riders glance at other riders. Or else they stare. Babies and old people stare the most. There is not a rider who is not a voyeur of sorts, in the best sense of the word, although obviously there are many different types of voyeurs and in varying degrees, with as many preferences for subjects as there are ways of looking. Yet, if I were to suggest to that woman sitting two seats away that she was a voyeur, she would certainly insist that she was just a casual glancer, and who am I to be looking at her anyhow?

"Well, now," I'd say. "You have a very good point. Did you study logic in school at any time?"

"No."

"I am merely trying to get you to see that you are a voyeur."

"Voyeurs are dirty people. I am not a dirty person."

"I can see that. You look very clean. But you still are a voyeur in the pure sense of the term. Would you prefer the English term, 'viewer'?"

"I saw you looking at me before." (She)

"And I saw you, watching me."

"Our eyes met." (Defensively)

"But we have nothing to do with one another. You are just another voyeur sitting in this train, and I am also a voyeur who happened to be looking in the same window at exactly the same time you were. Now, if you invited me to dinner, that would be a very different story. I might even go."

"But we have nothing to do with one another," she'd point out.

"You're right."

And almost before I knew it, we were two stations from the end of the line and I felt very hungry.

There were only three people at the noodle stand there on the platform: a man of average height, weight, and business suit, with his face bent over a steaming bowl, slurping the long white soupy pasta with great gusto; behind the counter, a bored-looking man of forty or so; and also there was me, Mai, looking forward to putting my own face in the steam. Funny thing, those noodles. We say they come from China, but the Chinese claim they never ate the likes of them, that if you wanted to eat real noodles you'd go to China.

I knew an Italian man who came to Tokyo on business selling Old World globes that looked every bit like leather but were actually plastic—looks nice in your library or office, you know—and he never even went near the noodles during his stay in the Orient. He said that if I wanted to eat real noodles, I'd go to Italy.

He was here for nine days. This was about four years ago. He had all these businessmen taking him out for dinner on the Ginza and Akasaka and such, and after each meal was over he said an early good-night to the business associates and called up this Italian woman who looked as I think Tosca must have looked— longish, wavy black hair, a proud head, large bosom, thin waist, and black fiery eyes that flashed when she talked. She was his business partner. She was not included in the men's invitations to after-hours business (which is, of course, when all the real negotiating takes place). Instead, she waited in the hotel for her partner's call. Then the two of them would head out into the city prowling after "decent food."

After the third night, they finally found it: a real Italian restaurant—"the only one!" they insisted, in all of Tokyo. And they went to this place, Angelo's (in the trendiest block in the Roppongi section, of course), every night right up to their last day in Japan.

"When we get home to Firenze," Tosca said to me, tossing her hair black, "we will be able to eat real noodles again."

I knew all this as it so happened that my boss, Fukuzawa-san, had me buying a fake-leather chess set from these Italians. That is, he thought I could charm the Italian businessman into giving me the set for a good price. I, however, was mostly interested in the great leather bag that this man walked in with every day, an exquisitely well crafted, enormous bag the color of mahogany, with the touch of a baby's skin.

When I asked him about it, he looked me straight in the eye and replied very tenderly, very simply, "I had it made."

Anyway, my boss wanted the chess set and had his eye on it

every time he passed the Italians' way to get coffee. We were exhibiting our trading company's wares in this grand old concrete structure called Exhibition Hall Building Number 4 during the Seventh International Good Housing Show. I was demonstrating electric space heaters that looked like fireplaces. The Old World globes and fake-leather goods were in a booth very near ours. I was one of the few Japanese who spoke English with any degree of ease, and so we got to talking.

When they told me they couldn't stand Japanese food and ate every night at Angelo's Italian restaurant in Roppongi, I was shocked.

"You mean you didn't like sukiyaki?" I was incredulous.

"Uckh. It has no taste." The man was vehement.

"Tempura?"

"Terrible!"

"Sushi?"

"It is uneatable!" Tosca stood, hands on her hips, eyes flashing wildly at the injustice of Japanese food.

So I laughed. And the two of them shook their heads and laughed with me. I was impressed by their intensity; they were impressed because I laughed. So we became friends. Weeklong friends.

We then had coffee together at the kiosk next to their booth, where the workers greeted us loudly with big smiles and "Welcome to HotCup!" They all wore uniforms that said "HotCup, Inc.," and in a singsong chant, they presented us with all the coffees we could order: Brazil, Kilimanjaro, Amerikan, Mokka, and HotCup's Special Blendo. When we gave our orders, they thanked us, turned around to the bank of vending machines behind them, and pressed a few buttons. Then they held their hands together and waited for the cup to fall down, fill up a quarter full with a thick black substance, and finally fill to the top with steaming hot water. The workers smiled broadly, swirled the cups of coffee with plastic swizzle sticks, and passed over our cups with napkins and a "Sorry to have kept you waiting!"

It was fun to get our drinks there, especially since the Italians thought it was all a big joke—it must be a joke, right? They kept pushing me about it, as if I had some secret insight to the whole scene—and they watched the HotCup people carefully throughout the Expo to try to judge their sincerity. Their conclusion, after one week, was that the workers were indeed very seriously going about their business of making coffee.

"What did they say?" my boss pressed me when I returned from the coffee stand.

"They said they eat at an Italian restaurant every night."

"No, no. What about the chess set?"

"The chess set? Oh, chess set. Yes, they said it was not real leather, but after the show they will give it to you for a good price."

"Oh, really?" My boss perked up. He was a troubled man, and it was nice to see him smile. "Hmmm! Tell them I am interested."

"I did."

"Why don't they cook at home?" he wanted to know.

"Why don't they cook at home?" I repeated.

"Yes, yes. Cook at home! You said they eat at restaurants in Italy every night. So I want to know why don't they cook at home?"

"Oh! Well, they probably do cook at home, but I meant that in Tokyo, they go to an Italian restaurant every night. A place called Angelo's. It's in Roppongi."

"Have they tried sukiyaki or tempura, I wonder," mused Fukuzawa-san. Suddenly his eyes lit up. "I'll bet they'd like sushi! I've heard that Italians eat squid. Well, what do you think, hmm? Why don't we ask them to eat with us tonight?" He really was a very thoughtful man, my old boss.

"Um, I don't think that's a very good idea. They've tried everything that foreigners are supposed to be able to digest. They simply don't like Japanese food."

It was a very odd look that settled on my boss's face. I tried to recall when I had seen it before.

"What do you mean, they eat only Italian food?" he asked finally.

There he was, demanding an answer, and at the time I didn't have one, so I just said, "Yes." We never discussed it again. However, since then, I met up with an Arab who lived several years in New York, and he told me that there were hundreds of Japanese restaurants in New York City and did I think they were there because New Yorkers preferred rice to hamburgers? Never, he said. It's because all the Japanese who work there would rather eat Japanese food than any of the hundreds of international food varieties available to them. I would have liked to tell that to my boss and see what he had to say, though obviously he knew this because he'd been to New York several times.

A large bowl of noodles, adorned with half of a hard-boiled egg, slid under my nose. While waiting for them to cool down, I suddenly remembered the only other time I had been given such an odd look by my boss. It had to do with travel. It had to do with the business about my passport, that's what.

"Mai-san, is your passport up-to-date? We might need to go to Germany to talk about those water heaters," he had said.

I blushed deeply. "I don't think you can help me," I had said. "If you insist, I'll go to the American Embassy and see what kind of red tape is involved. But it would take too long. Perhaps you should hire a freelancer to accompany you."

Not one to back off, he persisted, "Where are your Japanese credentials? Your mother is Japanese. Where are your papers?"

Where are your papers?

The words rang in my head. I was furious with him for asking, furious with myself for answering. My color deepened.

"I am not a Japanese citizen," came a voice at last, a voice clearly not my own, and clearly mine at the same time.

Could it be possible my boss did not know the laws of his own country? He was not a malicious man. Yes, yes. That was it. He was just beginning to see. I watched the odd look grow on his face.

It started in the left cheek, crossed over his eyebrows, and seemed to almost lift the skin off his right cheek.

"A child not born to a Japanese father has no claim to citizenship." I said the words aloud, formally, though I did not need to say more at that point.

"Sorry." He shook his head slowly. "Perhaps that will change someday."

"It's okay."

He went out of business eventually. First it was German burglar alarms, then CB radios from Texas, then back to German-made goods like washing machines, dryers, and printing machines—until he was beaten out by rival domestic companies that inexpensively copied and patented everything he imported at greater cost.

Still, he wanted me to continue working for him, but I hadn't gotten paid in three months and I wanted out. His wife, on the other hand, was doing exceptionally well in her trading company (selling Japanese goods), and when things broke down completely at our place, he left her and Tokyo and is probably living with some fraulein friend in Germany. Eating knockwurst?

3 | YOUTH KING

I felt tired after the noodles. Time to nap. Too much old stuff going through my head. Something about this Christmas thing here. Too many memories. I boarded another train, headed back toward the center of the city.

There was a draft somewhere in the car. Everyone had a seat. Long boots on women. Novels open, newspapers spread. A man picked his nose and dropped a crusty prize on the floor. Another man stared over the shoulder of his senior companion, who shuffled business papers on his lap. On a poster are girls in gay kimono, posing with piled-up hair beside the Christmas whiskey ads. They are eating New Year's soba noodles at a shop in Shibuya (with a branch store, "just as much fun," in Ginza). One girl's got the soba in her mouth, the one next to her is pointing and laughing, and one of them is about to put the noodles in her mouth but has stopped to wink at the camera.

Pages turn in the comic book to my left. Each page says YOUTH KING COMICS at the top. There's a fight in purple and a whole page of a man screaming, "*Aa-aa-aa-aa!!*" which—as the next page shows—is because another man with comets in his eyes and steel girders for legs is approaching him with a very long sword, and now he opens his mouth to reveal fangs that hang menacingly like stalactites. Suddenly, dark purple splotches of blood hit the page, and the head of the first guy is rolling wide-eyed away from the tip of the sword. Dialogue, dialogue between a group of men with glasses that have concentric circles where the eyes are, all except for the hero, who still has comets but with even more detail.

The pages turn faster and faster. There is a dark waterfront. A car pulls up. A whole page of black shiny car with arrows in the headlights. On to a room in a warehouse, and there, in a room blackened by shadows, is something behind the shadows. Ah. It's a girl. She's protesting—*"Iya!!!"*—and the men with concentric circles behind their glasses are tying her down with ropes. A number of purple pages with the men ripping off her clothes. She's bare-breasted and screaming. The hero says, *"Hee-hee-hee,"* and rapes her. She has a full page in purple agony. Then she says, *"Aa-aa-aa-aa!!"* like the first man, as her body is cut up and flung across the pages in spurting blood from limb to limb to lovely throat.

Not feeling well, I got out at the next stop to sit on the platform. I like to feel the trains go by. "Grounding," I call it. Like when you ground an electric appliance.

On the other end of my row of five blue seats was a young man reading comics and wearing *geta,* old-fashioned wooden shoes. He was dressed in a nice shirt with vest and pants, and had a coat slung about his shoulders. He didn't look up once. Four svelte, short-haired Shoppingbagwomen arrived in a group, all dressed up in gold belts. They were talking and laughing and wore high-heeled boots, with purses to match. One woman sat next to the young man and another next to me. Two of the women stood. They put shopping bags on the middle seat.

On the pillar between the two tracks was another new poster. It showed a smiling drunken man, coat and tie askew, with a briefcase in one hand and a box of sweets in the other, walking down the middle of the tracks. A big, growling train with a human face is bearing down on him from behind. The message reads: DON'T WALK IN THE MIDDLE OF THE TRACKS.

A train roared in, just like in the picture. The ladies all left.

The young man reading comics stayed. We were joined by a dapper young businessman in brown who took the middle seat. He crossed his legs. He moved closer to me. Then he uncrossed his legs, spreading them wide open. One leg stuck tight against mine. When he began staring at me openly, I put up my hood, closed my eyes, and counted out fifteen seconds until the train rushed in. I stood and waited for the door to open, knowing he was just behind me, clicking his teeth.

Chunka-swoosh! The doors peeled apart. A girl in jeans and a short furry jacket emerged. Then I stepped in—and he stepped in.

Then I stepped back out again, watched the doors close, *Shhh-thwump!*

He was gone. I waited until the next train pulled up, taking a seat in the Silver Seat section, which was reserved for handicapped and old people. Everyone always sat there anyway, I reminded myself. Besides, the lunch rush was long over and the car was only half full.

4 | THE MATURE RIDER

I have an address in Utah, and a phone number, too, which I have never called. There are two college girls who live there: they are my father's girls by his American wife. That makes them my half sisters.

Someday they might want to know about the trains, and about my becoming a Rider. Maybe someday they would visit Tokyo. Maybe I could be of some help to them.

I have decided to review my notes about the trains. This would be the logical place to begin. My notebook contains most everything they would need to know. It is a project I can sink my teeth into. Talk about trains and riding. Yes.

I suppose I couldn't be a rider if I were prone to motion sickness. But I'm not—nor do I have claustrophobia, subterranophobia, or misanthropia. All of which points to my being a perfect rider. I was, you can say, destined to be here now, going about my riding and enjoying the plastic seats on the platform and eating noodles for lunch. Things are much simpler now. My life before this is just that: a former time, a former experience, a not totally unrelated way of living, but a time behind me, and that is where it should stay.

I am a rider of trains. Riding is what occupies my time most. I tried communicating this telepathically to the woman who sat at the opposite end of the car. Her eyes were half-closed, revealing perfect thin lines of black eyeliner along the edge of the lids. Her mouth was drawn in a small, full, red shape, and her hair was piled upon the top and back of her head. She wore a formal kimono of plum and white and gold, so she probably was somewhere around forty-five; in jeans, she could easily pass for thirty-five, I thought. Her bundles said *wedding:* in her lap she carried a small, compact purse made of plum and gold tie-dyed silk, and at her side, occupying a seat, was a box covered by an enormous purple *furoshiki* (a scarf used to transport parcels) with ocean waves patterned in reds and oranges and blue.

There is much to learn from watching other people.

And there is much to explain about my favorite trains—the abovegrounds of Tokyo first, as those are what I rode long before the subways; the only other trains I rode were along the eastern coast en route to Kyoto (school trip), and, of course, to and from school.

All the aboveground trains are similar and yet none are alike. The green line is light and gay, the blue is dark and foreign, the yellow is slow and familiar, and the orange one fast and businesslike. They all travel through the main downtown sections of Tokyo, and though there are plenty of other trains around town, these are the most traveled and the best known.

No two riders ever agree exactly on the nature of these trains. However, out of these four, the best train—without contest—for getting most places downtown and also, consequently, the best train for sheer watching is the green train, which makes a large loop around the center of the city. As I said, it is light and gay. Even when it's dark outside and the trains are filled with drunken people throwing up on the floor, the green train is somehow cheery, and so you see how special it really is.

In fact, the green line is very exciting visually because of the scenery outside the windows, including all the important buildings one should see in Tokyo, like the Tokyo Tower and the Keio Plaza Hotel and the Shinagawa Skating Rink. Also, of course, the lights of the Ginza and the big posters and two or three stops away the neons of Electricity Street and then across town you can see some of the grass in Meiji Park.

But what makes the green line even more exciting is the incredible variety of traffic: riders of all types, nice new coats and worn old coats, hair swept up, hanging down, curled tight, short, long and stuffed under hats, and people with girlfriends, boyfriends, lovers, husbands, wives, children, babies, friends, grandparents, fellow workers; and, as is often the case on any given train, people by themselves, being quiet, falling asleep, talking to themselves, watching other people, avoiding other people, leaning on people, doors, and armrests, reading, looking for discarded newspapers, dreaming. Not that other trains are so terribly different, but just by virtue of its convenience—its popular destinations—the green line winds up with the most potential for interesting riding.

Another good point. Because it goes in a circle, you never have to worry about falling asleep and finding yourself heading way out into the country with no familiar billboards or buildings or train-yards, only rice paddies stretching neatly past concrete housing structures and small clusters of houses with laundry hanging. There's nothing wrong with the country, I suppose, but nothing much is happening there when you consider less and less people get on and off the train, station by station, until you are practically left alone in the car staring at some old woman dozing with her mouth open. Nothing but telephone wires above the rice paddies and schoolgirls giggling and schoolboys hitting each other with their caps . . . *thwap!*

I suppose I just get tired of the country, sort of angry even that people call it the country when it looks like nothing more than a city with rice fields. That the people are country folk may be true. What they live in is not country.

Perhaps if I had fallen asleep on a train and awakened to find real country, just the railroad tracks and green everywhere, lush and growing, amid groves of trees and water rushing along, and twigs crackling underfoot, and live birds dipping and diving . . .

Perhaps then I would feel differently. But, as things are, I prefer the green train, which takes a big circle around the big city with all its familiar people and streets and noise.

That is, I *used* to prefer the green line. Even now I ride it once in a while, but it's been a year and a half since I've ridden it with any consistency. When I had work, I rode it. Who didn't? And later, when my work ended, I continued to ride it—every day, in fact—but still I never saw the same person twice.

I switched to the metropolitan subway lines quite by accident, actually, and since that time—only subways. I think the green line became too airy for me. There were too many open-air stops and there was less permanence to the green line than, say, a subway line where people seemed more committed to riding, more inclined to stay in a car and less free to jump into the open air and away forever. There was something about the weather, too, that made the outdoor train lines seem so vulnerable and unprotected: gray weather and rainy windows, or windless days with glaring sun.

For many reasons I began to enjoy the subways more than the aboveground trains. Probably their consistency is what pleased me most. No weather ups and downs, no special indications regarding time, no street noise, few changes in temperature. . . . In many ways the subway is ideal. And I think all mature riders eventually come to that conclusion. The station dwellers, those most venerable experts on all station doings, wouldn't be caught dead on a platform above ground except for a morning browse through the cans; they live only in the underground passageways.

On a very fortunate day of riding and testing out and comparing subway lines, I discovered the red train, a private subway line. I noted how the seats were springy but not hard, that the upholstery was of a tastefully chosen, deep red fabric, worn in places and more so on some cars than others, but retaining a certain class that appealed to me. The silver bars lining either side of the car had smooth, triangular-shaped handgrips hanging from them, the old-fashioned kind that look like ivory ornaments and not so obviously plastic as the newer models. The silver bar armrests were placed a bit high for my taste, but I later grew used to them not as armrests but as rests for my head. When I am tired, I turn slightly to one side, prop both forearms up on the bar, and form a nice pillow for sleeping. The seats themselves are long, and face each other, unlike many newer seats, which are just the opposite.

The rest of the train is cream-colored except for the floor. Ceiling, seats, radiating units, walls—all are cream. Accent is provided by the passengers themselves. Red, silver, cream, and people.

The red subway is not as old as, say, the silver line, but neither is it young. It has roots but is not decrepit—on the contrary, it has all the vibrancy of a new train without appearing eager; it has vintage without mold; it has class without snobbishness.

There is a steady clientele, of course, including a good number of executives and well-groomed office workers, both men and women. And between rush hours, there are more Shopping-bagwomen on the train than on any other line in the city. There are little tots with mothers, students, jobless men, freelance people carrying portfolios, old women and old men, and, in general, leisure traffic. There are few young toughs, few right-wing demonstrators, few glue sniffers, and few suicides. Somehow its very gentility makes it a better place for people to watch each other.

On the green train line, the one that circles around town, there are always troublemakers of some kind. Drunks, militant student groups, men exposing themselves, ladies swearing to themselves, lots of suicides in front of the train (so much so that they've imposed very heavy fines on the families of the deceased for damages caused in holding up the trains), and pretty much of a rough crew all in all. Some of the right-wing demonstrators can be very nasty, picking on foreigners as they do, usually young American kids, and telling them they have to get off the train and so forth. They specialize in the dark art of intimidation, making everyone nervous, even when no one will be riding for too many stops anyway, such being the nature of the green line.

One day, though, while riding, I heard a very impressive speech—well, it was sort of a speech and sort of a song—on that train. It was made by a tallish, thin man in his late twenties who stood near the doors and made no move to sit down, just swayed with the train, and in a tenor monotone named what he thought should be done away with in Japan. Over and over he chanted:

> *Mitsubishi, Mitsui, Marubeni,*
> *These* zaibatsu *continue today,*
> *Robbing the workers,*
> *Robbing the people.*

The *zaibatsu*, I remembered from studying economic history, are monopolistic corporate giants. The thin bard repeated his chant three times and fell silent for a full minute, then began again, changing the words only slightly. He'd insert the names of other large companies in the first line.

Other riders looked uncomfortable. They closed their eyes or pulled out reading material. The whole train was quiet except when he began to sing. Boarding passengers got on noisily, but, hearing him, stared quickly, then looked away and forgot what they had been saying. Detraining riders got out quickly and breathed sighs of relief out on the platform. I myself began to feel spooky after a while and got off.

So much for the green line. That was when I was closing in on a major decision: which line to make my own. I kept coming back to the red.

There was only one problem, one true danger, with the red line. That is when the non-troublemakers themselves all become unruly at once. It happens very quickly, and I have witnessed it firsthand only once, with Fukuzawa-san. This happened during the strikes.

Being a private train, the red rarely—if ever—goes on strike. And because the other trains tend to go on strike all over the city all at the same time, riders from other lines travel this one when that happens. The day Fukuzawa and I got caught in a strike, people jammed each and every car from front to back. I remember we laughed about it, and Fukuzawa had just said to me, "It's some miracle we got seats, isn't it?" Then all hell broke loose. There were so many people trying to pack themselves in that the doors wouldn't shut.

In a split second I could not find Fukuzawa at all; elbows and backs and buttocks crushed in, surrounded me on all sides. Black wool filled my face, and I struggled to turn my head, even a fraction of an inch, just for one small breath! But I couldn't do even that. The train began to move. Somebody screamed, "I can't breathe! I can't breathe!" And the call screamed inside my own head, *I can't breathe!*, within my fast-blackening world, and then I heard a voice screaming back in battle cry, *Try, Mai! Try! You must free a nostril, just one nostril, one little corner of air!* I felt myself spiraling, out, out, out into some other space. The last thing I remember was a gigantic crashing, splintering sound, as the windows blew out.

Fukuzawa told me later that he was forced to drag me across the tops of others' heads—others who had failed to regain consciousness—in order to get me out at the next stop. I always wondered how he was able to do that with three cracked ribs.

My injuries were minor, by comparison. A few cuts and scrapes and a sore neck, mostly . . .

Isn't the risk of a major danger under unusual circumstances better than continual trouble at normal times? After much deliberation and close comparison, I chose the red train as mine, the one that felt good to me almost all of the time.

5 | EVENING TRAIN

Remembering that Italian girl. Sorry she left this city. Perhaps I'd have become close friends with her. We'd go to Angelo's together and one day I'd say to her, Say, you look like Tosca! I always thought so, but I never told you. You are so alive and vibrant and I am so closed. Let's have another bottle of wine and tell each other everything, as blood sisters do.

The train was warm and quiet. From above, the lights sent a dim, hazy glow around the seats. The car was nearly deserted. We stopped, the doors opened. Someone got in at the other end. The doors closed again. A low hum came from the speakers, and the cars moved forward heavily. *Clackety clack clack, clackety clack clack clack.* Soothing. Like rain at night.

There was a radiator under the seat gently blowing heated air against my calves. And the seats! They were lush red velvet, elegant, rounded, and soft, with stainless-steel silver armrests. I ran my hand over the exquisite fabric, savoring the plush feel, and sank back into the cushion propped up behind my back.

Ah! What could be better? Not the Riviera in the sun, not Hokkaido in the fall, not Bali nor the balconies of Madrid. None of them could measure up to this!

I felt truly relaxed. Totally, completely relaxed. Indeed, I hadn't felt so relaxed ever. Thoughts flowed freely, swiftly. There was Tosca again, with her flashing, indignant eyes, and there was my old boss sitting in his office with the door open. "Mai!" he'd call out. So I'd go scurrying in from the outer office to see him, pen in hand. "Sir?" I'd say. "Mai, can you speak Greek? I'm about to call Xanthos-san and I was thinking maybe you could make the call for me, hmmm?" "Sir, I told you last time you called Athens that I don't speak Greek. I'm really very sorry." "Oh," he'd say, "you did?" "Um-hum." "Oh, well, would you mind speaking to Xanthos for me? Your English is so much better than mine, and you know he doesn't like to make any mistakes—neither do I, really—and it's about quite a big order, hmm?"

"Sure," I'd smile. The secretaries behind in the outer room were giggling to themselves. They always had good laughs about my ability to speak Greek. So I'd call Xanthos and he'd say, "Oh, it's you again, is it? When am I going to get to meet you?" "I don't know, sir." "Well, let's get on with it." "Yes, sir."

God, those weren't bad times at all. I suppose it was because we all got along so well. Fukuzawa-san was well liked. He had a very innocent melancholy about him. A bit moody, he was. He once sat at a party I gave and drank in the corner all night, listening to everyone who came by to talk with a sweet, calm smile on his face and loneliness so full in his eyes that everyone eventually left him completely alone.

That party! It was Christmas Eve—three years ago, I guess—and, as Sabena announced to everybody, the seventh anniversary of my relationship with Nobukazu. We had about fourteen people over to trim the tree and drink hot-buttered rum and eggnog; only two people were actually putting up decorations. Sabena and I were keeping the rum hot, and ourselves and guests full of same. Meanwhile, the living room was so noisy with music and laughter and old tales of holidays past that I didn't think to glance over the party for unhappy guests. After all, we were all pretty much long-term acquaintances and it was Christmas and there was plenty to drink and there were the hosts to make toasts to.

So, with two drinks in my hands, I went sailing through the room toward the tree to see how the trimming was going, and there he was, my boss, sitting with those eyes of his and a broad smile on his face for me.

"Happy Anniversary, Mai."

"Thank you." I smiled. I sat down on a cushion next to him and offered one of the drinks I was holding. He shook his head, grinning, and pointed to the bottle standing behind a potted fern.

"Cigarette?" he asked, holding out a pack.

"No, thanks. I don't smoke."

"Is that so? Oh, yes, I guess that's so. Come to think of it, I've never seen you smoke."

"Um-hum." I smiled.

"What year is it?"

"You don't know?" I asked.

"Your anniversary. What year is it now?"

"Oh! Yes, of course. It's the seventh. We've been together for seven years." I looked around for Nobukazu. He was laughing and slapping the knee of the man who sat opposite him—Sumio, a jolly sort of older man who worked next to him in the same office.

"Lucky number, seven. May you have seventy-seven more!" Fukuzawa-san lifted his bottle, waited. I lifted the cup in my left hand. Together we drank.

And somewhere in there amongst the small talk about Nobu and me and the office and the other secretaries, I asked him about his wife, just something simple, like, "It's a shame Madame Kyoko couldn't make it? How is she?" And he looked at me with an extraordinarily puzzled and searching expression. At length he replied, "She's fine, I think." At the time I remember thinking it was a strange sort of answer with a look to match. I interpreted it as loneliness for his wife, who must be staying home with the kids this Christmas Eve. Anyway, I reasoned, since she and the kids had never been abroad, Christmas probably meant little to them, mostly a glittery affair with a decorated cake. My boss, on the other hand, no doubt had a strong nostalgic attachment to the holidays, having spent several years in Germany. All night he had been looking at Sabena's marzipan and *zapfenkuchen* with such longing that no one wanted to be the first to eat it, just so he could keep feasting his eyes. Perhaps he regretted his wife's indifference to Christmas. . . .

In a way, I was not far off, but I certainly never suspected the truth, not even when everything was practically written all over his face for me to read: that they had separated long before, that they remained married for appearance's sake, that they had lunch together on occasion mainly for business purposes and for the morale in both—separate—offices. When I finally found out all this, it seemed ridiculously obvious. But at the time, for whatever reason, I could not see my boss very clearly. Had he been more honest with me, I would not have felt so haunted by his eyes that night. As it was, I excused myself from his side shortly after mentioning his wife. The conversation seemed to have ended; he was simply drinking and smoking and appeared capable of caring after himself, with the aid of a taxi to take him home later.

So I joined a lively corner in the hallway where Sabena was telling German jokes in English. When she got to the punch line, she'd switch over to German, and everyone roared along with her and poured more drinks. German beer appeared suddenly, causing wild yells and a quick chugging contest to clear cups for the great delicacy. The listening crowd looked like a small summit meeting, what with German, French, Japanese, English, and Americans all gathered in one place, none of whom ever really got any of the jokes except the Germans, but never mind. Sabena had a manner of telling stories that made everything she said somehow understandable. Her mellow, contagious laugh kept rolling and rolling along, pulling in the small laughs all around her till the group sounded like one great whooping tide that lifted higher and higher until it crashed out onto land in a dozen different directions.

Sabena herself never once suspected that no one understood the specifics of what she said. I know because I asked her once about it and she appeared very insulted. Anyway, when I think back to that party, and others like it, I tend to think that the People of Industrialized Nations (PINs, I call them) do have more in common than other people of the world, and the democracies in particular seem to get along. Perhaps that was what I had in mind when I hooked up with Nobukazu in the first place, and I still think it is sort of true, but, PIN or not, Nobu could not communicate with me at all. Four months after that party, we separated for good. I began to know about our future on that very Christmas Eve.

After all the guests had rolled into their taxis, I put out the bedding and got under the covers. Shivering, I rubbed my hands together and moved around as much as I could stand to in an effort to warm up. God, but it was cold! I could hear Nobu in the next room clinking glasses and crumpling papers. He was tidying up. He was always tidying up. I decided not to lose patience. He'll feel better if it's neat, I thought, so I'll just wait right here. No need for me to join him if I don't want to do it just now. And although it was our anniversary, I told myself, it was just another day, and I must not expect anything different.

But then I began to think of all the endearing things I could say to Nobukazu to remind him of my delicious womanly self, to kindle his desire for me, call him to kiss me passionately, delicately, his sweet burning lips separating my lips; my hands holding his face his chest his slender hips, and turning on my side my breasts full and warm, nipples just touching his chest lightly, tantalizing; and I circle my hand around the top of his thigh and around under his muscular buttocks, squeezing, pressing my breasts tightly against him now, my knee caressing the full length of his inner legs, my whole body quivering with excitement at bringing him to such excitement, and he, unable to bear the teasing anticipation, cries out for me. My head tilts back. . . .

In darkness he came in, folded back the covers, and got into bed. He settled himself down, drawing the full length of his body next to mine. I closed my eyes and his familiar smell fell around me, sank into my nostrils. It was like wheat tea, pungent and damp. Nearer he drew. His face was suddenly upon mine. He kissed me once on the cheek, squeezed my breasts with one hand,

and then, with the same hand, he reached straight down and began pumping me hard on the crotch. With a strength deep beyond myself, from a place that felt powerful, deep, and darkly red, I grabbed his hand at the wrist and threw it back to his body. I heard his wristbone crack against his pelvis.

"Why did you do that?" he cried. And he began kicking me, his long legs pulling up higher and higher to gain momentum, kicking my calves, my thighs, my buttocks, my hips, and then the backs of my knees as I struggled to turn away. I heaved myself up out of bed, but not before he had time to grab my arm with both hands, jerking me down again. His fists crashed one after the other into my shoulders and then darkly into my chest, harder and harder until I found myself choking, fighting for breath.

I do not know how long I was screaming, "Stop! Stop!" and finally, "Stop for Christ's sake!"—or even what language I was using—but just as suddenly as he had begun kicking, he was now standing back from me, fists still clenched. I was clutching my chest with both hands, curled up, crying, "Stop! Stop!"

"Please be quiet," he pleaded. Strained eyes pleaded from the broken mask. "Please be quiet, please be quiet." Eyes filled with hurt and anger. Heavily, heavily, he drew in rasping breaths. Was his throat broken? I could see that he was going to cry.

I could not say anything, could not think of anything I could say to him anymore to make him understand. We had been through it all before: it was a "blood matter," he said. A woman of my background is not "true Japanese," and therefore we could not truly communicate; we were essentially different. Irreconcilably different. So he believed. That had to be it. What else could it be? He insisted that my "cultural blood" was the source of our problems. He said, "Our rivers can never mix and flow as one." He was quite poetic when it came to our troubles.

Of course, I knew that some of what he said was right. Our "rivers" would never mix and flow together because he could not release the dam that walled him up and kept him a closed, secretive person, and when he did release, it looked like this. It looked like a broken woman lying on a bed and a defiant, hostile boy with tears in his eyes and fists clenched. Only now, finally, there just wasn't room for us to cry together and make deep, satisfying love to each other afterward: there was only a man standing with his knuckles showing white in this darkened room and a woman named Mai lying on rumpled bedding with a searing pain in the chest and bruises swelling up on her legs and shoulders. I saw so clearly that night. We had no real connection to each other. There was nothing there. Nothing to mend. Nothing to save.

In fact, now that I was riding the trains, not only was there nothing left of my life with a stranger, but no job, no boss or his marriage, no fat jolly Sumio or any of those people at the party. Even Sabena was gone. They are all gone.

If there were one person I would like to see again, I think it would be Tosca. Ah well. I closed my eyes and sat very still. The low drone of the loudspeakers continued, providing the bass below the tympani—*clackety clack clack, clackety clack clack clack.* Wasn't this the life? Wasn't this the best there was? The velvet red train in the dark underground with the night outside above the ground, late-outing riders, golden light, warm air, and quiet peace.

I felt drowsy but didn't want to sleep. Who was with me? Who was enjoying this quiet, close time with me? A woman in kimono, asleep. A young couple, also sleeping. Three drunken men sprawled across seats, and a half-drunk salaryman reading a street handout. His cheeks held the bright red dots of alcohol flush.

Back to the young couple; they seemed so tranquil. Her pretty head on his shoulder and he with his head falling forward. Beneath a plain brownish wool overcoat, her legs were held close together tightly, and I suspected she wasn't asleep. Her hands held a purse on her lap, and there was something else there too—a bag, perhaps. Yes, a shopping bag of some sort, folded underneath her purse. The boy looked to be about twenty-two and wore his hair curly but not very long. His hands were folded in his lap.

They weren't really sleeping at all. They had gone to a movie, one of those romantic Alain Delon pictures, and they watched the love scenes barely breathing, excited to be so close to each other and watching this together. She ached to be embraced by him and he by her, but neither moved, feeling clumsy and shy. And later, when the movie was over, the lights went on and she laughed and said it was good, wasn't it? Then they got on the train and one by one the other riders got on and they had had to sit close together to make room. . . . But then the other riders departed, and they continued to sit close together on the warm red seats in the hazy golden light. She could feel the heat from his thigh through the woolen overcoat, and her own thighs were electric. Still she sat not daring to move, and she . . . felt drowsy and closed her eyes, dropped her head, fell slowly sideways, sleepily, found his strong, youthful shoulder. Her hair fell forward in a glorious black sweep and covered her face, her face which was flushed with his nearness and the pounding of his heart. They pretended to sleep as the train rumbled along through the tunnels in the night.

And in the window directly opposite me was a woman of some age, dark hair visible under a hooded coat, a wide face, pronounced cheekbones, smooth, clear skin, a set chin, and eyes that looked rather like those of the Italian woman who sold fake-leather Old World globes.

6 END OF THE LINE

End of the line. The conductors on duty walked through the moving cars as the train pulled into the station, rousing sleeping passengers, shoving the shoulders of drunken men.

"Last stop. Yo! Last stop."

I live at the end of the line. Every night it is the same: sometimes the conductors can't do anything to get the passengers off except roll them out the doors and onto the platform. They carry men off like sacks of rice, one conductor at the head end and another holding the feet. Then the lucky stationmaster who runs the station at the end of the line has to figure out how to get rid of the bodies deposited on his platform.

Tonight there are more bodies than usual.

"Can you believe it?" Ogino-san, the stationmaster, spoke to me as I passed by a sleeping, suited fellow sprawled out on the concrete, glasses askew. "He's lucky if he still has anything of a bonus left."

"Why do you say that?" I paused. "Is it so expensive to get into a bar these days?"

"Hell, no," laughed Ogino. "Wallet snatching. End-of-year bonus time, you know. A helluva lot of wallets snatched these past few days. Most of them full of cash, and the wives mad as can be, come down to the station and want to know have we seen their husband's wallet?" He shook his head. "Never used to be like this, as bad as it's getting."

"Well, good night then, Ogino-san." I took one last look at the swollen red cheeks of the drunken man, who reeked with the sweet-rotten smell of whiskey, who slept so peacefully. He was probably forty, but I could easily imagine him at fifteen, so smooth was his skin.

But Ogino was already talking on his two-way, telling one subordinate to get down there and another subordinate to flag down a taxi. It appeared only three of them had pulled night duty; anyway, if it weren't for the drunks, the station would practically run itself.

Outside it was snowing. Snow! It was a rare occasion. Car lights flashed golden rings in the street, and two cabbies called at me from across the street.

"Tokyo Station?"

"Kirijoji Park?"

"Ginza?"

The one that called out Ginza grinned at the first speaker, then turned away as I shook my head.

She lives here, said Second Cabbie.

Oh yeah? First Cabbie turned to smile at me. A big silver tooth gleamed in my direction.

I didn't have to listen long to their talking at me. Both of them had seen me here before: they just needed something to do. I heard them as they hailed the two train attendants with body in tow, saying, Him again?

Sure, I know where he lives.

In a city of millions, I thought, they know where he lives. Imagine!

The men's voices chimed good-naturedly together. Yo! Let's get in, fella. Ho, he's a heavy one. Don't drop those glasses! And the four unloaded men loaded the loaded man into a cab. After taking this last one home, said First Cabbie, I can get loaded.

Laughing voices rang all the way up the street behind me.

When silence finally came, it fell around my head and settled into the pavement, along with the snow. I turned the final corner toward home.

7 | EMIKO

Black wet and no ice in the center of the street; no cars either. *Gatcha gatcha gatcha!* Ivory pieces cracking together, men's voices rumbling from the second story of a mah-jongg parlor. A light shone out. Watch out for ice! Thin patches were forming at the edge of the road in shallow pools. The street was all circles and shade and blocks of falling light: soft golden circles at the base of street lamps. Shallow oblongs of fluorescent light from the bank of vending machines. Cup Noodle tobacco hot coffee cocoa sake prophylactics batteries fresh milk Coca-Cola orange juice girlie magazines and bags of rice in three grades. A cat scrambled out of a garbage pail and darted across the street, scaled a wall, disappeared.

Still the snow fell.

One more golden circle and I would be home, another rectangular signpost glowing with the English lettering that said ROSE MAISON.

There it was, a concrete wall, and high old pampas grass still uncut from autumn, a low little wall directly below the building where bottles collected overnight, and now a little hump that was sitting in the dark on the wall.

A little hump?

I slowed down. Yes, a little hump with little boots that just reached the ground, and a wool hat with a tassel, and a big overcoat, making what appeared to be a little girl into an extension of the wall.

"Komban wa" (Good evening), I said, bending down.

"Komban wa," she answered. She seemed to be looking me over.

"Cold, isn't it?"

"It's not so bad." Her voice was clear and strong. I guessed she was about seven. She peered past me down the black street.

"Uh—what are you doing here?" I asked, stepping aside so she could see better. I looked down the street too. There was no one in sight.

"I'm waiting for my mommy. She's a little late, I think. But she'll be here soon. She always comes for me here." She kept her eyes on the road.

"Oh." I gathered that she didn't particularly want me around. As I turned to go in, though, she looked at me again.

"Do you live here?" she asked. Her teeth were chattering. So she really was cold, after all.

"Yes," I said. "Mind if I sit down and wait with you?" I went to sit on the concrete wall.

"No, but . . . You don't have to wait with me, you know. I come here every night. I leave my house at twelve-fifteen like my mommy says, and she always comes at twelve-thirty." She got up suddenly and looked down the street again.

"So she's a little late tonight, that's all. She'll be here soon," I said.

"You don't have to wait with me."

"Tell you what," I said. "I'll leave as soon as I see her coming, okay?"

"Okay." The little girl paced around and kicked a stone into the street. It was very quiet. In the distance we could make out the lights of Tokyo Tower all lit up. The snow was beginning to taper off.

"Have you ever been to Tokyo Tower?" I asked.

"Of course. My mommy took me there and we went all the way to the top. She always takes me places. I went to the zoo, too."

"Which zoo?"

She didn't answer.

"Did you see the panda bears?"

"Of course! And the tiger and the birds with a thousand eyes." For a moment her eyes shone as if the peacocks were there before her on the sidewalk. Then she sat down again, frowned, and gazed down the street. Always the same direction.

"Then it's Ueno Zoo." I pulled my muffler around my cheeks, leaving just enough of my mouth uncovered to talk. "If there were pandas, it had to be Ueno Zoo."

"Ueno Zoo. That's right. I forgot the name." She turned to me. God, what beautiful eyes she had! She stared directly at me for a while, just watching.

"My mommy has a coat like that, too."

My coat? I looked down.

"She has a coat like this?"

"Well, not exactly like that. But almost like that. It has a hood like that, only it's not brown."

"What color is it?"

"Sort of red."

"Oh."

"Do you have a watch?"

"No, sorry. But I'll bet it's close to one. The trains stop running at twelve-thirty, and since I took the last train here, it's probably about—let me see—probably got in at ten to one or so. Oh, my, I think it must be at least one o'clock."

At that she twisted her gloved fingers together, over and over, though she looked quite brave and calm whenever she turned her face toward me. A car came around the corner in the opposite direction. The small figure jumped up and peered at it. Meanwhile, I was halfway in the door of my apartment house as I'd promised, but the car sped by and continued without slowing once. The child watched it until it disappeared. I hesitated, then walked out to her.

"Hey," I called softly. "Wrong one, huh?"

She only shook her head with her back still to me.

Just then the lights of another car appeared in the distance, this time in the right direction. I started to go back into the building, taking care to stay out of the light over the entrance.

The car slowed, pulled to the curb opposite Rose Maison. The little girl remained motionless and waited. It was a foreign-made car, an expensive model. A man reached over and opened the door on the passenger's side. A woman in kimono and with piled-up hair got out, looked quickly across the street, and said good night to the driver.

"Mommy!"

The woman adjusted her stole, then waved as the car pulled off. The little girl hugged her big coat around her and danced excitedly as her mother crossed the street.

"Emiko!" And although the woman scanned the area in all directions, she apparently did not see me in the shadow of the wall where I waited, barely breathing, until the two of them—Emiko and her mama—were well on their way down the street.

8   ROSE MAISON

Outside the Rose Maison, all was still. On the sidewalk, new snow had almost filled marks left by other night travelers. I took one long last look down the street at the small set of lightly ridged tracks next to slender, smooth-soled prints like those made by miniature skis, footprints that could be drawn only by a woman's *zori*.

I let myself in.

There were three Chinese meat dumplings out on the table in my kitchen. I ate two and went straight to bed.

The next morning I awoke in the same room I'd slept in for ten years—seven years and four months of those with Nobukazu, two years and eight months by myself. Mai-self. My-self. I wrote it on a pad by the bed. It was my name, Mai. Mai-self.

Why had they named it Rose Maison, anyway? There wasn't a single rosebush, only two young plum trees planted the same year we moved in, the same year it opened for occupancy. We had been lucky to find such a new place, so close to a subway stop and all that.

Nobu's mother had liked it, but his grandmother complained about the lack of greenery. That and the cold concrete hallways— she didn't like those. The two women argued about it.

Concrete is ugly, said Grandmother.

It's strong, Mother would say.

It's so dingy-looking.

It won't fall down in an earthquake. (This was a dig at Grandmother, whose beautiful old wooden house—the one in which Nobu's father was born—collapsed and burned in the Great Kanto Quake of 1923.)

There was always something to argue about. Taken separately, the two were much easier to deal with. But it was always a strain when they came to visit.

No more visits. Thank God.

I rolled over onto the tatami and then stood, found the main light switch, and surveyed the room. There was no furniture, only a clock on the floor along with pads of paper and two wooden knickknacks from Hokkaido. They were carved bears, a mother and a cub, which Nobu and I had bought as a souvenir on a visit to the north country. This morning, standing here in the predawn, I couldn't imagine why I had kept them all this time. More trinkets. No purpose to trinkets.

They can go to the trash, I decided, and I stuffed them deep in the pocket of my overcoat. The coat had served as a top quilt during the night. Underneath it lay the silk futon, a wedding gift from Nobu's supervisor. It occurred to me that I might fold up the bedding and actually put it into the bedding closet for the day. This was funny. Doing housework of any kind seemed a funny idea.

In America they don't hide their beds, I thought. Perhaps I should be living in America, with a big high bed, loaded with fat, fluffy pillows. I would need a new name. Maybe I should call myself Rose. Rose Maison. I laughed out loud about that one.

In this good mood, I prepared for a new day of riding.

9 | QUEEN OF ALL REVERIES

It was cold.

At six in the morning there were no shopkeepers out as yet, dousing the sidewalks with basins of water. That would happen about eight or nine o'clock. Everything on the street was closed and walled. There were no birds; only gangs of dogs ripping apart plastic garbage bags and trotting off sideways as dogs do.

I think they were looking for the sonofabitch who keeps loading dishes and appliances and stuff on top of the garbage cans.

The light said SUBWAY and down the stairs I went, taking care, two flights of concrete, into the long hallway and up to the ticket machines. I debated. Should I show my pass or buy a ticket? Should I buy a ticket and show my pass anyway? The ticket-taker boxes hummed mightily. Ticket-eaters. They take your ticket and give it back with a hole neatly bitten out. Certain bugs do that on canna plants. I bought the cheapest ticket and sent it through the box. *Thwurp!* Gone. *Ahhhh—zing!* Up it came all warm and with its hole punched. Always, I might add, in the same place, that hole.

The man in the office looked sleepy. He nodded. I nodded. He pointed out the new flower arrangement in the glass box by the escalator going down to the platform. Ah, I nodded. It was pretty—pines with snowy white flowers whose name I did not know.

I waited for the train to come.

I heard it first, a low rumble in the distance, and as it rumbled louder, the sounds separated into steel on steel: steel on tracks, motor steel, and whistle steel. Closer and closer, and then I could see the lights, one appearing to illuminate the front car and the other lagging behind. The lights came closer, lined up. The train eased in to a slow stop, and when the doors opened, I got on.

Only two young skiers in the whole car, young men sitting side by side, their skis propped against the upper baggage rack. They watched me get on without a pause in their conversation. Something about their next train connection to get to the trains that go way up north to the snow country. The pitch of their voices was sweet, unsettled. Maybe they don't smoke enough, I thought. It was really very pleasant, to hear them speak. So I listened for a while, and closed my eyes.

I slept through the entire morning rush.

I dreamed I was back in the garden with Nobu's mother, talking. She looked just as she always did, wore the same navy kimono with the gray belt that pictured tiny fans around the borders. She was speaking earnestly to me about Nobu from her doorstep, and as I listened, I reached out from time to time to lift up the leaves on her rosebushes, searching for aphids.

"Nobu is no ordinary man, Mai," she said gently. "He always liked foreign girls, you know?" The rosebushes were totally infested with the little green bugs. Ants trailed up and down the thick stems, little black dots against green.

"Look at these," I said, pointing. "You'll have to spray the bushes. They'll kill your roses before long!"

"Why, no, dear," laughed Nobu's mother. She stepped down into the garden and lifted a leaf, folded it back. "You pinch them off—like this!" Carefully, she began squashing the little bugs between her right thumb and forefinger, one by one. Green juices dripped from her slender fingertips. "Go ahead—you can do it!" she called to me. But I was stepping back . . . back . . . back. . . .

I jumped up as an old woman squeezed and poked her way

into the seat next to me, saying, *"Sumimasen, sumimasen"* (Excuse me, excuse me). One of her parcels had fallen into my lap. Her grabbing it back had startled me out of my dream; my hood was down, and I had dropped my own bag on the floor. People were staring at the old woman with her cloth-covered bundles, and staring at me as well. Quickly I pulled my hood up and moved over to give her room. But it seemed like the more room I gave her, the more she needed. Soon I was dead against the rail, and she was still pushing. I decided to stand for a bit.

The old woman continued to adjust her bundles. She reminded me of a woman who sold vegetables where my mother lived. Almost completely toothless, old Yasuda-san would always call out the same thing when a customer approached: *"Moyashi?"* (Bean sprouts?) "I've got beautiful *moyashi!*" She'd stick her whole hand in the bucket of bean sprouts and hold out a bunch in her fingers, dripping with water, for the housewives to see. Even though you came for just carrots or a turnip, somehow you arrive home with bean sprouts too.

It was a very good start for a day, I thought. By noon a poem came and I wrote it on the wall in the bathroom of Kozai Station next to an umbrella that expressed eternal love between Yoko and Tet-chan. It went like this:

THE FEAST
Oh put us all together
In a cozy warm space
With light to illuminate our faces.
Give us eyes that open and eyelids that close,
Coverings for ourselves and our belongings
And we will feast on each other.

Its inspiration I attributed to the mother of two little girls whom I saw on the train just after I awakened. The three of them sat on the end of a row, next to a schoolboy who wore a high school uniform and looked awfully sick. He held his briefcase stiffly on his lap and stared straight ahead. Probably going home.

The little girls had *Pierre Cardin* printed on their kneesocks. They were clambering all over the seat and playing with colored bits of paper which they folded and held up to their mother, who nodded and looked away.

She stared into the window opposite, right through the old man dozing there in the radiated heat. The littler daughter began to punch her mother on the arm. Lightly at first. Dark little mischievous eyes! Mother ignored her and continued to stare. The little one hit harder and harder. Dark intense eyes! She pulled back her wee fist once more and struck again, and, at last! the mother turned suddenly and made a great wince of pain, and placing a hand on the abused shoulder, cried, "You've hurt me!"

Her daughter drew back to sit quietly on the seat—such a tiny thing she could barely dangle her feet—looking neither surprised nor hurt nor sorry. She didn't look anything. The mother turned back to the old man dozing; but everyone in the car had seen the incident from start to finish and stared fixedly into their own airspaces. And the mother's reverie was indeed broken.

I used to think that mothers never really forgot about their children, even for an instant, never could separate themselves from the products at the ends of their umbilical cord. And fathers? They have another attachment. Sabena, merry girl that she was, had a father who beat her mother bare-fisted with heavy, thudding blows; they separated when she was eight. Luckily. She told all in confidence of how she herself witnessed a nasty, nasty fight, in the dining room I think it was, in which her mother had no clothes on and was trying to flee and—at the same time—keep quiet so as not to wake her daughter, though children generally know about these things anyway or see them firsthand.

Poor Sabena. Poor Sabena's father and mother. Sabena could

never see her father in any other way, stuck in time as he was by his own doing. When her father moved away, she didn't meet him till many, many years later when he was already an old man with an aging second wife. And Sabena's father, although he never wrote letters, always sent her a birthday card and present, always lingerie: some pretty nightie, a slip, lacy things. She dreaded her birthday and made sure she gave all her friends extravagant presents so she wouldn't get just the one gift from her father when her birthday rolled around.

Did he forget that he once had a daughter whom he fathered, fed, and cared for? I think, yes, he must have forgotten. Mothers, too, must forget sometimes, in another way, for their reveries cannot always include their children. As Natsuko once told me, Natsuko the Queen of All Reveries, mother of two beautiful little girls:

"You know, I sometimes forget I have another child." This she told me two months after her second was born. We were sitting in her kitchen, midday sun streaming in on the table.

"And though I love them, I always think of leaving everything and going off to the dunes on the western coast. I went there during college—by myself. Do you remember the pictures? It was so restful. There is nothing but the dunes, mountains and mountains of sand. And in the distance"—she said, sweeping her hand out, just missing a pot on the stove, so tiny was her apartment—"the ocean! As far and as wide as you can see!"

How expressive her eyes! How earnest! How gay her laughter, like the melody of spring brooks running over rocks.

Did I remember the pictures? Ahh. There must have been thirty photos or so, twenty of them just dunes, exactly as she said, mountains and mountains of what I imagined to be golden hot sand, fine-grained, burning in the day and cool in the evening, gracefully sloping, sensuous and powerful. The rest were pictures of the sea head-on, nothing in sight and nothing new but the crest of the wave. She said she took them in early morning before the people came to ride the camels. Camels? I asked. Yes, and ponies, too, poor things, they ride them to death nearly.

Two photographs of Natsuko at the dunes. She must have asked some tourist to snap them for her. One photo I remember especially well: of her standing on a sloping mound of sand with dune grass growing to the side. She is leaning most of her weight on one leg and holding one hand to her head to keep back her hair, which appears to be blowing around in a strong wind. She is wearing a dress that comes to her knee, and it is clinging to one leg and blowing out from the other. She looks pensive. . . .

Where was she now?

If she were the same as ever, she would take her daughters by the hand and board the long train to the land of the dunes. If she were to do that, wouldn't I meet her there? If she could free herself from her husband, that pathetic little engineerman who defecates on her poetry and darkens the hollows in her cheeks, where would she be now? Why haven't I called her in all this long time?

"Mai! Have you been well?"

"Very! And you?"

"You haven't called in such a long time."

"Nor you."

"I thought you were busy. . . . " Her voice wavered.

"I have been."

"And Nobukazu?" Her voice was controlled, but I sensed her anxiety, like a knife at my throat.

"I asked him to leave." There was a long pause. I swallowed hard.

"What will you do?"

"I thought we would go west and see those dunes you always told me about." I laughed. "What else is there for me now?"

"So silly, Mai! Ho! You are more of a dreamer than I!" She laughed, and it was music: a flute and tinkling piano keys.

"Oh, no! Never! No one can compete with you, Natsuko. You are the woman of summer, the Queen of All Reveries!"

And together we laughed into the phone at an old joke until there was silence again.

"And Tomio? How is that husband of yours?"

"He's the same. Although things seem a little better with us now. I got him to quit that temple he was going to. I told him that his daughters were suffering while the priests took all our money. I said to him, 'What would the Buddha have to say about priests who drive in American-made cars? Has God given them permission to drive these boats down the streets while we are hungry at home?' They really took everything he would give, Mai, and it was beginning to be not just his bonuses but part of his salary as well. I finally called his parents and got them on my side, and we all had a talk with him."

"He agreed so easily?"

"Of course not. But his mother is strong, you know," Natsuko said slowly. "She can do what I cannot."

"I'm glad for you," I said, and I really meant it. I had a hard time even being civil around Tomio. He brought out the worst in me. Even as I said Hello to him, and How are things at the company, privately I was always thinking: Fat little clone. Then I would feel guilty for thinking bad things about my best friend's husband. But finally I stopped feeling guilty at all. I decided he must be an android. He could not be a human, after all—he just appeared human in form. What else could I think of a man who gave wads of money to a corrupt temple and a mere pittance to Natsuko and the children?

At one point I stopped pretending I liked him. I think Yuko must have been three at the time: she was at the age where she was climbing up onto everything in their apartment, and I distinctly remember peeling her off the balcony rail as she called down to one of her playmates in the playground nine stories below. I told Natsuko what I thought about his behavior, especially with regard to the money, reminding her that most husbands turn over their entire salary for the wife to handle. I even told her I called him a fat little clone to myself, and she was truly shocked. Oh, but he's kind, Mai, really! He's very gentle with Yuko. . . .

Things changed for the worse when the second baby came along. Another girl, Sachiko. Natsuko's voice was severely strained when I spoke to her over the phone. I guessed she was getting no sleep, what with nursing and all. And I suspected Tomio was turning cold toward her, for whenever I asked about him, out of politeness more than anything else, she sounded near tears. Fat little clone, I swore at him privately, I'll bet he blames Natsuko for not giving him a son.

Natsuko called less and less frequently. When I saw her finally, one pretty day in Meiji Park, the little ones in tow, she confided in me that she did not like to have sex anymore; fortunately, he did not bother her about it often. God, I said to Natsuko, has it finally come to this? Do you remember when we were just out of school, and the way we went out dancing, and. . . . Yes, I remember, Mai. But it doesn't seem to be me. Does it seem to be you when you think about all the men you had hanging around? Yes. No. I don't know.

Metallic undergrate, fold, lift up, stair. I took a walk on the escalator. It was weird: there were no stairs anymore at this stop. No stairs, no ramps, no elevators. Just escalators moving smoothly, swiftly, folding stairs up and under and around again. Up escalators and down escalators. Little Yuko would have liked this stop, I heard myself say.

Or did I? Did I say that out loud? Maybe. Better check that stuff. People look at you funny if you talk to yourself too much. I'd seen the stationmaster looking at me funny—even at my own stop, at the end of the line.

This was an impressive set of escalators, what with ups and downs both and three people wide. If you got off at the first landing, you could change to the yellow line or the silver line. The last landing going up was the change to the above-ground trains, and after that only exits leading to buildings and daylight. There were some nice restaurants on that upper plateau, but they all specialized in businessmen's lunches, costing a great deal more than noodles. Breezes swooshed cold wind down the exit stairs from the street. Cosmetics girls with matching white wool suits came down the stairs from the cold, clutching elbows and wrapping their jackets around themselves tightly. They straightened their hair in the mirror of a coffee shop window and sauntered off arm-in-arm. They looked at first one restaurant window, then another. Must make good salaries to choose so blithely.

The upstairs restroom was crowded. I headed back down the escalator.

Middle-aged couple three steps down. He pinched her behind. Then he looked around to see if anyone had seen him. Oh! She squealed, and she slapped him lightly. Then it was her turn to look around to see if anyone had seen him pinch her and her slap him. No one had, of course. They giggled together.

Down the long corridors past station people sleeping on wads of newspapers. They're very smart, those station people. Sleep during rush lunch and eat later when the restaurants dump their leftovers. Makes for a quiet meal, first-class cuisine in this station. Nothing cheap about it. No noodles here.

People were standing in lines at the ticket machines. I stood behind an old man with a runny nose who kept dropping his change purse. *Click, click. Click, click, clickety click, click, click.* Some ticket-punching conductor had a good rhythm going. *Click, click, click, clickety click, click, click.*

Hmm. Odd. Why should there be a ticket-puncher in the station? There hadn't been ticket-punchers for years.

The machines that punch tickets must be broken. I turned away from the machine and followed the lovey couple through a makeshift wicket. *Click, click, click!* Only a pro from the old days could work up a rhythm like that! He didn't sound the least bit rusty, either. Must be like riding a bike, ha-ha.

The man on a stool with the metal clicker just kept taking tickets, didn't once look up. I smiled at him. He took the ticket which I had handed wrong side over and flipped it over to the printed side. *Click click!* I put it in my coat pocket with fifty-two other tickets. Counted them in the morning, I did.

Fifty-three now.

Together we waited for the train. How often does the train come? The woman asked the pincher, leaning over to peer at the schedule against the post. Oh, about every two minutes and ten seconds, I thought.

Oh, about every three minutes, he said. He put his arm around her. She looked up at him. They continued to snuggle once inside the train, against the doors. There weren't many seats, but someone had just vacated one at the end of the car. From there I could see the people in all of five cars as we groaned around the bends.

I recalled that I hadn't yet been to the toilet.

Voices from a nearby conversation made their way into my ears.

"Have you seen Sugi's exhibit?"

"Sugi's exhibiting? Where?"

"Pentax."

"You're kidding. Pentax Gallery?"

"Really. You remember those things he shot in Europe—the kids?"

"You mean running through the fields in Germany and the streets in Italy and Spain, whitewashed houses and stuff. Color, right?"

The First Cameraman nodded. Second Cameraman shook his head.

"Oh, come on," said the First. "What's wrong with that? It's a great theme. Very popular. Well done." He adjusted a black leather camera strap that was hanging around his neck; there was a film canister taped to it.

"Sure, he's got a few nice things. The girl with the balloon, you know which one I mean? She's holding the string and half the balloon is in the upper right—bright red—and there's nothing but sky surrounding her and outlining her head. Her legs are cropped off just below the knees. Very effective. I agree he's good. But that stuff in the Pentax Gallery? There's better around and you know it."

Second Cameraman wore a suede jacket. Underneath it peeked the lens caps of two cameras, just sort of poking out between the buttons.

"You're talking about your own stuff, I assume." First Cameraman smiled, prodding his friend's elbow. "What is it you've been doing after hours?"

"Are you serious? What time do I have outside of that goddamn studio? Simpering little pampered models who act like, if I don't tell them each they're the loveliest little pieces of ass ever to stand in front of my camera, they can't work with me for some reason. Can't hold a pose, can't do anything creative, wait to be told to wriggle their noses—God! I hate this fucking business."

The speaker stood up and walked over to the door. First Cameraman followed, gathering leather bags and a muffler.

"Okay, okay. You hate the business. So do a lot of people. But fashion is money. Money to do other things." First Cameraman pressed his friend. "You're doing something now. What is it? Something with Mari?"

Second Cameraman smiled. We were pulling into a station. "Where are you going?" he said.

"You know where I'm going! I thought we were going to drop by the agency."

"That's right. But, hey, let's go for coffee first." Second looked at his pal and laughed. "There is something I've sort of been working on. Can you look it over for me?"

He glanced at his watch as his glove went on as the doors opened as I got out, too. I followed them to the escalator, but nothing more was said. They stood on different steps and started walking before the escalator had reached the top.

Nobu had a habit of doing that. It seemed like he just couldn't wait for the top of the escalator. Had to run on ahead. Almost like it was important for him to do that.

All men do that, said a voice inside.

No, they don't, called a voice, also from inside. It was a familiar voice. A firm, gentle voice that called up a picture with hot flood-lights, a time past:

I had eaten lunch, as usual, with my boss, in an underground mall. We were on the escalator, sharing a step. We talked and joked all the way to the top. The escalator walkers trudged steadily upward, in a passing lane, as we stood to one side. I felt myself standing next to Fukuzawa-san. I knew his height by the shoulder that nudged mine. I was aware that when I wore this pair of high heels, he and I stood absolutely shoulder to shoulder. And now I was completely flooded with his presence—could feel the sleeve of his trenchcoat on my arm, heard the rustle of fabric. I barely heard what he was saying for the slightest crush of fabric. I did not know what he talked about, but I knew his body temperature. Though I knew my feet were standing on steel, some-how I felt only him.

One voice struggled to push through, saying, *Come on, Mai. Get back to reality. The man's only talking to you, for crying out loud. Get back to those steel steps, you crazy girl.* It struggled against the temperature I felt from Fukuzawa, bullying and pushing, push-ing, even as my cheeks flushed full with love. Struggled against an-other voice that said: *This is good. This is right. Be in this moment. Love this time and this place.*

I heard those struggling voices again, tried so hard to hear which was which. I knew the whole scene was happening again, and I savored it. I could hear: *This is good. This is right! This is!*

But in the end, crashing through, like a bull that bursts through the gates into the arena, heading straight at the toreador, the voice, the thought formulated fully, at long last: *How could this be? Look around you, Mai. See where Mai is now.* And as I stepped off the top grate of the long escalator, alone, cool air whipped crossways on that next level, like some kind of trade wind run-ning perpendicular to the current. At that moment, I hated that mind-voice, that authority out of nowhere, and I desperately loved the one that had said, *No, they don't, Mai,* and, *This is good*—so gentle, so firm. I loved the journey it gave to me, and I wanted it back. But it seemed very gone.

Flushed and with my heart jumping against my chest, I ran straight for the bathroom. Had it been fifty or five meters away, I couldn't get there soon enough.

10 IN THE MIRRORS

Safe in the lavatory. A woman stood back from the mirror, fixing an eye. Her face followed the width of the mirror and then went straight out the door. All the booths were open.

Above the toilet paper, ZOKO was pen-scratched in the paint. Ah, Zoko! Zoko had red hair down to her thighs and green paint on her eyes and breasts. She was a rock star. People said she was really a man.

I lingered inside my booth. It was too quiet, though. I was beginning to wonder where everybody was. When I got out, I checked the other booths for graffiti. It was just the usual stuff. I had this urge to try out my American name. Yes! What better test for a new name!

Back in the first booth I scratched it on the door in uppercase letters, using a Swiss penknife that my father had left behind. The little knife had a red case, and it was one of the few things I'd kept of my father's. I liked it because it was something he had actually used. It was useful, and I liked useful things.

ROSE MAISON

It looked pretty good. Just above it, marking an earlier time—the very first time, in fact, that it ever occurred to me that I, too, could write on a bathroom door—was my own name. It read: MY NAME IS MAI. HIGH MAI. MY HI. Then there was my graffiti signature: a little bowl of steaming tea, with the lid lifted off.

This is what it looks like:

In school we would have been expelled for writing graffiti. At least that's what the nuns told us. No one ever tested them to see if they were bluffing. Too bad. I would do it differently if I had to do it all over again, I thought.

The station sinks were shiny, with strands of hair that stood out on the white enamel. Whose hairs? Whose hairs? Coarse and black. Thick as a horse's tail. Straight and long.

"Do Not Comb Hair Over Basins." All right. I'll just wash my hands, thank you. Oh, please do. But when you wash your hands, you will wash the hair away down the drain. And so? It'll get clogged, of course. The drains will clog, and before you know it the toilets will clog, too, and won't that be a scene? Yes, it will. Is there some connection between the drains of the sinks and the drains of the toilets? When the water flushes downward swirling away and cleansing all of us, where do the pipes lead? A central pipe, I'm sure. Yes, there must be a central pipe, I'm sure. Yes, there must be a central pipe, and all the water with hair that snuck through the clogged drain and wastes from lunches and coffees goes through the central pipe, a big pipe. Then there is a

vat of sorts, a separating vat that needs no workers at all, it's completely self-operating. Waste is filtered through, and water, boiled of organisms and recycled back to the sinks and toilets. Of course. How silly of me not to know. I've often wondered where all the waste goes afterward, and it being a very delicate subject of discussion . . . I thought it emptied into Tokyo Bay, but that's not so? Not at all.

We did have a Western toilet in my school. The tall nun who was the English teacher once complained to the school director that the girls were squatting over the Western toilet instead of sitting down, and that the seat was always dribbled on. *"Girls are to sit properly on the seat and not squat,"* said the notice that was circulated. This was, in our eyes, a declaration of war. So we let it be known—through the appropriate channels, of course—that it was the elderly Home Budget teacher and her bosom pal Miss Tokusato, the Japanese Composition teacher, who were dribbling. After all, most of us had had Western-style toilets in our homes for years, and being young as we were, wasn't it Eminently More Probable that the above-fifty-and-nearly-Senior Citizens were the ones doing it?

I can't say that I thought about sewage in high school, but I am wondering about it now. What do they do with what is left behind in the big vat full of waste? Why, they burn it. They make gas for the cars and factories. This gas provides the power for the water to go back into the pipes and flow up a fifty-two-story building as well as down into subway bathrooms. Very simple, efficient, and closed. Closed? Closed.

Two young women clicked onto the tiles with boots. Traffic at last! They carried shopping bags.

"I'll see him today, you know."

They moved into separate booths.

"Oh really? Is that where you're going?"

"Yes. Where is it you have to go—Hankyu Department Store, right? If so, we can get off at the same stop." Toilet paper rolled *ratcha gatcha.*

"Not Hankyu. Pilo's—the boutique. You know it." A toilet flushed.

"Anyway, I was thinking if you wanted to meet him, I should introduce you, don't you think?" A door opened. The other toilet flushed. Out came one of the women. She washed her hands and took out a white handkerchief from her purse. She stood back and looked at herself in the mirror. She glanced at me. I opened my bag on the counter and looked through for a brush. She got out lipstick. The other girl called from inside the booth.

"Really, I was thinking of going for a long time. How long do you think you'll be there today?" She came out and clicked over to the sinks. She ran right into me. "Oo! I'm sorry!" she said, then walked over to the end where her friend stood combing her hair over the sink.

"It's okay!" I answered, smiling. "Happens all the time. It's my brown coat, I think. It's very plain, blends in. Of course the hood is nice. In fact, it's my favorite part. I can sleep quite a sight better with my hood on, you know."

"How much does he charge for an initial appointment?" The Second-One-Out said in a low voice. She reached for her purse with wet hands.

"Take mine." Her friend passed the handkerchief. She noticed the sign taped to the mirror and moved back away from the basins.

"It's not so bad if you have insurance. You have it, of course?" She peeked at me in the mirror.

"Of course."

They hurried to leave. Bags shut, boots zipped, scarves folded.

Lots of things go on in bathroom mirrors. It was how I met Natsuko, actually. We were in a bar bathroom. I remember the sink was shiny jet black and there were towels provided. Pink towels. When you were done with the towel, you folded it back up and put it on the counter. A girl wearing purple eye shadow was standing there at the mirror holding both hands to her cheeks when I got out of the booth.

Her cheeks were flushed and her eyes shone brightly. She looked straight into the mirror at herself and said, "Wow. I think I've had a lot of whiskey this week. Monday night, Tuesday night, Wednesday night, Thursday night." She counted by nodding her head up and down, and then turned to me in the mirror. "It is Thursday, isn't it?" she asked.

"Yes, it's Thursday," I answered. Then I laughed. She looked like she didn't mind drinking whiskey four nights in a row.

She smiled back. She wore all black—some kind of soft knit jumpsuit—with long knotted beads of purple and black. Her hair was wavy and long in the front, but cut very short in back. It was jet black. Later I was to see that in the sun it looked almost blue.

"Do you come to this bar often?" she asked.

"Yes, I do. Quite often. A man I'm dating keeps a bottle here."

"You're sitting in a corner, aren't you? Near the piano?"

"That's right. Why, where are you?"

"Oh, wow." She laughed and waved her hand. "We're way near the back. Toward the entrance. When you come late you can hardly get a decent seat."

"That's really true lately. It's gotten popular, hasn't it? But— I think you've been here before?"

"A few times. We usually go from place to place to place to place to. . . . " She giggled as she repeated the phrase for a while.

"Whew!" She stopped giggling to roll some lipstick on and then moved her lips around and around and around. Then she laughed again.

"Too much whiskey! Every night this week. Let's see, Monday, Tuesday, Wednesday, Thursday, and tomorrow, too! Oooh, wow." Cupping both hands to her cheeks, she held her face close to the mirror. "Think we'll head on to another bar. Yes, I think that's what we'll do." She turned to go.

"Are you enjoying the music tonight?" I asked quickly.

She rolled her eyes back and sparkled them at me. "Do I like this music? Do I?" She threw her head back and laughed. "If I had a seat like yours, honey, I'd be here every night with my boyfriend and my little private bottle, too!"

I was very glad she was drunk when I met her. Otherwise, she never would have told me that she liked my seat, for, as I found out later, she was very reserved with strangers except when she was drinking. As it was, I invited her to sit with us since we had plenty of room where we were. She accepted immediately. She moved up to the front with her girlfriend, the two of them carrying their own glasses, a bottle of whiskey, and a pitcher of water with the waiter protesting all the way behind them until I waved him away: he backed off like a spanked puppy. Natsuko met Nobukazu then and introduced her girlfriend—Mitsuko, I think. Someone, it turned out, who just liked to go drinking in the nicer bars around town, and wasn't such a close friend after all.

Nobu had given me a look like, What are you doing now, Mai? when Natsuko and her girlfriend came trouncing up to the table like that. Natsuko nearly tripped for ogling the pianist—he was quite a fine jazzman who'd cut his first album just around then. I told Nobu not to worry, she was a friend of mine, and Natsuko turned just long enough from the pianist to introduce herself as "Natsuko, hi, we just met in the bathroom."

Nobu couldn't take his eyes off her after she smiled at him and sparkled her eyes. He was very happy to have the company, as I was too, and only then did I realize that I had been needing company at our table for a long, long time.

That was a lucky bathroom break.

Which brings voyeurism to mind again. If we were not voyeurs, we would never have any interest in looking at other people in mirrors, and so we might not meet them. Natsuko looked at me directly because she wanted to look, like all other women in the bathroom. That she talked to me was the accident. When we found that we were totally compatible, it was not an accident. When I married Nobu, a year later, it was a matter of course. When she married Tomio, it was because she didn't really care who it was, just so long as he was quiet. She married to please her mother, whose health was failing. That, too, was a matter of course.

That she was in love with Nobukazu for all that time was something I never forgave her for, not even when I finally asked him to go. Who needed this pain? Who needed to marry, after all? How often have I wished that Natsuko had told me herself, long ago! How different everything would be today. . . .

At the time my marriage died, I became nothing. I was nothing. It was not just the death of my marriage, of my being married—but that I could not even turn to my closest friend for solace, for I saw her as the riptide that pulled relentlessly to the death. Angry, I mailed back to her every poem she had ever copied down for me, every letter, every trinket, every piece of evidence that spoke of the long betrayal.

Of course I went back to my mother's when the last bitter words were spoken—between Nobu and me, that is. I didn't even want to look at him. I certainly couldn't stand to see him pack. He didn't even know where his things were in the apartment— and I would have had to stand there resembling the good wife I did not feel like, locating his belongings, whatever they were. Let him find them himself, I said to Mama. I need to come to the country.

She said, "Come ahead, Mai."

Everything was as it had always been there, except for two things. Mama had tired of modern appliances, for some reason, and refused to use even an electric rice cooker. The rice had to be boiled and attended to before each meal. She insisted on doing this herself.

The other thing was Mama's cat. This cat had given birth to three kittens out back in the gardening shed, and according to Mama, had come back to find them all gone, dead. Probably the tom got them, she said woefully, or maybe they were poisoned, ate something in the shed. Mama crossed herself, then kissed the cross that hung around her neck.

This event happened the day before I arrived. So all week

long that cat walked around the property, calling with the most godawful howl, looking for the babies, her milk-laden underside swaying heavily from side to side.

I cried for a long time. Every time I thought it was over, I'd hear that cat yowl again—and I'd cry again. Mama said it was a sacrifice—the whole situation of the cat's, that is—set up for my sake. She said it brought on the "blessed cleansing." I believed her. Everything she said made sense after I was there a while. And I sure didn't want to think for myself. I was too tired.

"My body aches today, Mama."

"That's from the weight of carrying your pain around," she'd say.

One morning I got up ahead of her. I cooked the rice the old-fashioned way, as Mama had been doing, in a blackened rice pot with a heavy lid. You had to stay there to watch it so that it did not boil over in the beginning or get too dry toward the end of the cooking. It wasn't so bad. I used the time up chopping scallions and slicing tofu for the morning soup, and fed the cat outside on the garden path.

From that point on, I made the rice for every single meal, right up until the time I got back on the train for Tokyo. I felt a lot better.

In Mama's bedroom was a carved Kamakura mirror, a hand mirror. I remember looking into it the morning I went back to my job. I had been gone a month. I guess I wanted to see if I looked as different as I felt. I wanted to see if my trials had marked me or scarred my face or showed anywhere in any way, and picked the truest mirror in the house to look into—the one with the least distortion. That was Mama's mirror. I loved it dearly, remembered the smooth feel of the lacquered wood from my childhood days, from those special occasions when Mama allowed me to touch it.

On this day I knelt, picked up the mirror carefully, and turned it over to see the picture I had been avoiding that whole while. Dark, ashen-colored half-moons showed beneath both eyes. That was the only obvious sign the outside world could see. But there was some other difference that caused me to stare a long time. Was it in my cheeks? Was it the forehead? My mouth? I could not pinpoint the location of the change, yet changed I was. To this day I cannot quite put it into words that describe it well, not even in my own mind.

Mama said, "To me, it looks like the light is falling on you in a new way."

"What do you mean, Mama, in a new way?"

"It's a good way," she said. "I can see your features more clearly."

"That's because I've lost weight," I teased her. "It sharpens one's appearance."

Mama took my sarcasm as a sign of health, and sent me on my way.

I wondered now, Was it a matter of light?

The memory pulled me back to look closely at myself in the station bathroom. That was over two and a half years ago. Had the falling light changed? In the lavatory mirror, I was me again. Pushing back the hood, I pulled my hair high into a ponytail, held it with one hand. Then I lifted my eyebrows as high as they would go, and determined to practice my new name out loud.

You want truth? I said to Mai. *This is a moment of truth.*

To make it real, I pictured myself on a plane to Los Angeles, talking to the sandy-haired athletic man seated at the window. He said his name was Ryan, and held out his hand to shake. So it was now my turn.

The mouth in the mirror said, "Hi. My name is Rose. Rose Mason."

The name was not working. I began again, with a small change.

"How do you do? My name is Rose—Rose Maison."

But in my head were these words: "No smile came forth for Ryan, nor did sun's light forgive her darkness."

I tried once more.

"Hi. I am Mai," I said aloud, watching the word work on my mouth.

"Ma." It parted my lips.

"Ee." It caused a smile.

"My name is Mai," I whispered, and walked out.

Others whispered behind my back.

11 CONFESSIONS OF A SCHOOLGIRL

If I were to share my life with my sisters, I could tell them every-thing: I would tell them what I see, all of what I see, and all of what I know, or think I know.

My sisters: if I tell my whole story to you, you can choose better—to like me or not like me. Therefore I will not hide any-thing from you or pretend to be something I am not. At least, I will try. . . .

Without thinking, I had gotten back on the train. I had to laugh at myself, how automatically I function. After all, I disembarked in the first place to eat lunch. That is, I thought I did. It seemed a long time ago. Next stop was Kudono Station—two stops from the Mimata changeover. Well, I could wait and switch trains if I wanted to, or I could eat right here at that boiled noodle place on the platform. . . .

Decided! (Hunger often wins, doesn't it?) Quick! Before the doors close! I thrust my brown bag between the doors and they jerked open for five seconds—just long enough to hop out over the gap between train and platform. How experienced I had be-come. What an expert Rider!

I like this noodle shop. I eat here probably ten times a week. A group of vagrants have posted themselves at the other end of the platform. Probably waiting for everyone to leave so they can attack the noodleman's trash.

"What'll it be?" called a voice.

"One portion, please," I said.

The noodleman served me from his steaming vat of brown soup in which he was cooking fresh batches of pasta.

Ah, yes. There's that poster that went up four days ago. It announces a movie coming at New Year's. Even as I slurped soft, fat udon noodles into my mouth, I watched the men go by and stare at the ad. It is not in the trains, but you can find it in the stations on posts at transfer points. It is of a girl in high school uniform: middy blouse and navy skirt, white socks, and a school emblem. She sits with her top coming off and her skirt hiked up. One finger is in her mouth. She looks rather scared, and completely naive. White panties peek out from under the blue. She appears to be waiting.

She is nearly life-size. Lots of people pass by her. This noodle stand is directly opposite the poster, so my vantage point was excellent. And I could tell you that women do not look at this girl. They go straight past her. They breeze by her, using their peripheral vision. They talk past her. Go around her. But never have I seen a woman stop and stare at her or even glance directly at her.

Men, on the other hand, do all of the above. They breeze past her, miss her, talk past her, stop, stare, look her up and down, laugh.

What was I doing back in high school? I remembered all the taboos about wearing my uniform: Don't be caught dead in a movie theater with your school uniform on, or the name of the school will be soiled. Don't go to coffeehouses or bowling alleys or skating rinks, either. Don't wear white ribbons in your hair, lest the public think you are frivolous and "free" (translation: "loose"). Don't let your hair hang down—for the same reasons.

All of my high school days seem very mild by comparison with this poster girl. About the time my body began to change, in sixth grade and through middle school, I liked to read girls' comics. They were big, thick, pink-covered books made of recycled paper, about starry-eyed, long-tressed heroines who went to fabulous balls and received—oh gosh!—a kiss, from a tall, handsome man with a sports car. It was tremendously exciting when the kiss came . . . orgasmic, actually, in relative terms. I would go back to the page where the kiss happened again and again. But it wasn't really until ninth grade that I became fully aware how exquisite my body could feel under the hands of people other than myself.

There was a Japanese-American boy in the private school I attended in Tokyo. He was a junior at the time and somewhat of a baseball star on the school team. His father was Nisei, like mine, and worked for Sears. I had just started to wear nylons. All the other girls were wearing them since the sixth grade, except for those who had Japanese mothers like I did. (The other moms were international businessmen's wives, for the most part—Americans, Aussies, Brits, Scots, and so on.) Although your mom's nationality was not completely the deciding factor, to be fair: some girls with Japanese moms were wearing makeup as well as nylons in the sixth grade because they were afraid for their kids to be different from the other kids.

This boy was tall and broad-shouldered, and all the girls liked him. In the lavatories they conducted wars over him, but in front of the boys they were very reserved. He had a bit of a swagger from all the attention, but even so he was very shy. I knew him because all us Japanese-American kids hung out together. We used to make fun of our Japanese mothers, but we drew the line if the white kids tried it. Then we were very defensive. "Don't you talk about my mother that way! Your mother can't get off her bean curd white ass long enough to put a lock on your refrigerator!" We'd say that because lots of the other kids—the foreign kids—were fat.

Anyway, there was this Annual Sports Day in which the whole school took part, even the teachers who refereed and ran races. I was very good at table tennis and was in a match between my homeroom and another, a very big deal. So this boy showed up all hot and sweaty after his baseball game and stood in the midst of a whole group of rowdy boys. I was intensely aware of his eyes. And God, did I play!

I won. The crowd cheered wildly, and I got swept outside with all my girlfriends. We walked around, checked out all the other games, and finally, when the sun began going down, we went to rest high up on the balconies of the school building. The sun was still beating hot up there. I was sitting there with two girlfriends, trying not to go home, when this boy—well, I suppose I should say his name, Kazu—walked out onto the balcony, and said, "You look like you need a back massage."

I just sat there feeling his hands rubbing against the thin athletic T-shirt I was wearing, and I could feel the juices flow. God! I thought, he'll feel the hooks on my bra if he goes any lower, but he kept going lower and there wasn't a thing I could do about it. I broke into a mild case of hives around my neck; meanwhile my girlfriends, who were kind of suspended there with me, pretended to be involved in a serious discussion, not very successfully at that.

Naturally, from then on, it was much easier for me to dream in class. After all, it wasn't some princess-looking comic-book character I was dreaming around: it was me, Mai, with hair brushing my lower back, nice teeth, slightly pudgy ass, long and slender legs, and a nose with very little bridge. It almost didn't matter when Kazu was lured away the following year by a redhead in the same grade. I had that hot day to think about, forever.

Sometimes I thought about Kazu when I was loving Nobu. It's funny. Nobu's full name was Nobukazu, so I never felt very far from Kazu in the end.

Then, in the eleventh grade, I had even more to think about. Besides the nuns and the lay women teachers, there were only three men teaching classes in the girls' sections. One of them was the boys' history teacher and also, by default, the swimming instructor. The school, being privileged to educate many sons and daughters of foreign diplomats as well as business executives, had a pool connected to the gymnasium, and the head nun determined that we would all learn to swim every stroke—on pain of not graduating. In fact, we all graduated anyway, even the kids who never once entered the water—and there were a few of those. But we girls decided early on it was a painless experience. That was due to Mr. Dodd.

Mr. Dodd was not what you would call handsome. However, he was mildly famous as a model for coffee ads, because he had a beard and a mustache and sort of classical, British-looking, distinguished features with a scholarly air. I liked his quiet jokes and serious manner, and, as I said, it was not a painful experience for my friends and me to hop into tank suits and go swimming every Friday afternoon. He was a nice man.

When we threw open the heavy door leading out from the girls' locker room, Mr. Dodd would be doing laps. He was always doing laps. The class was huge—maybe as many as fifty girls. He would herd us all on the side of the pool, up and down the full length, and we would practice strokes first out of the water, and then in.

It was the second class of the crawl. Low paddle kick, one arm reaching, other arm pulling down and under, scoop the water, over and up, breathe on that side, face in the water . . . Reach! Other arm pulling down and under, keep kicking, scoop the water, over and up . . . Breathe!

I could not get the breathing. Which side to breathe on? Would it be enough air before I got the arm through the water and could breathe again? We practiced in the shallow part, all of us dunking our heads and trying to coordinate our arms. One girl bugged out with a stomachache. Some fifteen or twenty girls crawled ahead to the deep end because they already knew the crawl from country club pools or wherever. They got in trouble and had to come back and help the girls who couldn't do it. Mr. Dodd waded around patiently lifting arms out of the water, saying, "Girls, if you refuse to cup the water, it will flow right through your fingers. See? Cup the water, cup it!"

Everyone was splashing and trying and getting water up their noses. The old pros were alternately explaining and goofing off. Mr. Dodd came around to my spot and asked to see how I was doing. I showed him. He told me he had never in his life seen anyone who had perfected a more awkward way of breathing.

"Oh," I said. I had really worked to make it look smooth, but the truth was I honestly thought swimming was the most unnatural thing humans could do, and if it didn't feel right, how was I to know?

"That doesn't feel right to you, does it?" he'd asked, smiling.

"No, it doesn't."

"Try this," he said, and in the standing position he worked my arm through the air down and under, the other one reaching, and just as my arm came up from behind, he lifted my face sideways and said, "Now breathe!"

"Okay, I've got it," I said, embarrassed. I glanced around me to see who might be watching. But everyone had seized the opportunity as a good one to splash around or jabber on the pool's edge, so I was spared.

"Yes, but try it in the water this time," he insisted. "You won't sink because I'll hold you up."

As I lowered my shoulders into the water, and picked up my feet, he moved in to hold me around my middle, but instead of finding my waist he pressed his hand directly against my breast under the water. That large, strong palm on my nipple! That firm grasp, not letting go!

Quickly he moved the hand down when he realized what he had done. Both hands were around my middle then and I was feeling waves of heat from my breast flow up and down my body and my crotch was throbbing like mad . . . I was glad to have my head in the water.

Mr. Dodd himself seemed a little embarrassed by his mistake, and so I relaxed a little; then he helped me with my kick by propping a hand deep down to boost up my pelvis—"just for a moment," he explained—and I was nearly dying then as I felt his own throbbing against my outer thigh.

Mr. Dodd was not like the lecherous Father Elkin, who taught upper-class religion and who put his arm around our shoulders as low as he could get in class reading time. No, Mr. Dodd was a serious sort. I liked him even more after that class, but nothing like that swimming lesson ever happened again, and I was left only with my fantasies.

Somehow I became much more excited by that memory than I was by that big poster of the schoolgirl with her knees spread. I guessed it was just a personal matter, after all. Who's to say that another woman doesn't fantasize over a revealing middy blouse? I took a few minutes after my lunch to sketch out a woman fantasizing over a revealing middy blouse.

12

KAZE GA FUKEBA . . .
(IF THE WIND BLOWS . . .)

I had been traveling back toward the center of town, somewhere in the vicinity of Sophia University. An interesting couple entered the train about one stop earlier. She was tall and dark, with short-cropped hair. I guessed she was Australian or American. He was Japanese.

The pair ran breathlessly into the car where I was sitting, and stood above me. The boy slipped his arm around her waist. He peered over her shoulder as she pulled out a textbook and held it out in front.

"This is what I'm studying today," she said in Japanese. It was the kind of Japanese we call *gaijin kusai*—which means, literally, "reeks like a foreigner." Her accent was terrible. But it was not broken Japanese; the grammar was perfect. I was impressed.

"Whoa. That's one of those old-time sayings that doesn't make any sense," teased the boyfriend. "Do you really have to memorize it?"

"Yes," she said, making a face. "Word for word. The whole paragraph. The teacher is very strict."

"Go ahead. I'll help you if you can't read the *kanji*." (*Kanji* are Chinese characters used in writing; they're the tough ones to memorize.)

"It's okay. I think I know all the ones in here. But correct me if I sound funny."

"Okay, baby," said the boy, this time in English.

"*Kaze ga fukeba, mokeya ga hayaru,*" she began.

I closed my eyes to listen. If I wasn't mistaken, I had had the very same text in my Japanese culture class.

"If the wind blows, the basket shops prosper. This means, if a high wind blows, dust can fly into the eyes of men, blinding them, so that they are forced to become samisen players in order to earn a living, which increases the demand for catgut with which to make samisen strings, and as the cats get killed off, mice roam more freely, biting through household baskets that hold rice and other grains, and causing the housewives to purchase new baskets from the basketmaker's shop, who grow more and more prosperous as a result."

"Waah! That was great," said the boyfriend. He made no attempts to correct her unfortunate accent.

"Well, now I've got to think up something that has happened to me that I can relate to this," the foreign girl said, shaking her head. "It's part of our assignment. Can you think of anything?"

"*Soo ne* . . . Let me think a minute," said he.

She kept on studying the text. Then she cupped one hand against the boyfriend's ear. "Anybody thinking in there?" she joked.

"Hey, give me a minute. I don't see you coming up with anything yet."

At last he grinned. "Here you go. Perfect example. 'When gangsters fight, the ordinary man's child takes a cold bath.' " He looked completely pleased with himself.

"Wha-a-t? You're crazy," she said, punching him lightly on the chest. "How do you explain that one?"

"*Iya desu yo*. It's not nice. You won't like it," he laughed, shaking his head.

Several other passengers were listening in. Two men stared openly at the foreign girl's waist, where the boyfriend's thumb now gripped her belt tightly.

"Promise me you won't run off if I tell you." He pulled on the belt, mock-menacingly.

"Go ahead, I'm not scared of a crazy boy!" She laughed, showing perfectly straight white teeth.

"Well, you see. There was this thing on the news last night, you know, about these gangsters who had a fight. . . ." He paused.

Several people were whispering to each other now. I wondered what it was that everybody else knew.

"Yeah, go on," she urged him.

Noticing that the others were listening, the boy suddenly switched to English. He had a British accent. "Well, one gang cut off the hand of the rival gang leader and slipped it into a noodle-maker's soup. It was hours before anyone realized it, and they think several people actually were served noodles after that, at the bloke's noodle stand."

"No!" the girlfriend squealed in horror.

"Gross, huh? Well, those noodle stands might be controlled by gangs, they say, so people aren't too happy about risking a meal at any of those places, and we're gonna see all these blokes who normally eat out go home early to eat with their families. So, you see, since Daddy gets the hot bath first, now, the kids are stuck with the cold water!"

"Huhd." I heaved. I tried to get up, but I was wedged in solid. I tried to say "Excuse me" in any language, but all that came out from behind my palm was, "Huht. Huhd."

Half-digested noodles gushed up and out onto the floor, right onto the foreign girl's jeans and boots. She was screaming, trying to kick her feet and step back, and he was still stuck in her belt, and everybody was scattering on either side of me as I sat there, retching. I could hear the metal doors to other cars opening and thudding shut as riders escaped the reeking car.

I would have said I was sorry, but I was cold and clammy, and I wasn't finished throwing up.

At the next stop I grabbed my bag, and, stepping over the dark yellow pile in front of me, I swayed, grabbed the door, and hurled myself onto the platform.

I could not even walk to the bathroom; my legs wobbled like soft tofu. The lights of the station spun around and around. I sat down on the platform seats, hung my head down.

Eventually, my stomach settled. I got myself to the bathroom and washed out my mouth. I felt much better.

No more noodles for me.

I took care not to get back on the train until I no longer felt the slightest bit queasy.

13 | Ordinary Men

It was an ordinary man who pinched an Australian girl in a train one day. And she, being of strong build and will and pride, turned to kick him in the crowded car. She was attacked by him and other ordinary men in business suits and cardigans, stripped of her clothes, and able to flee only after the train (interminably) reached the next stop.

Perhaps Elizabeth (that was the name of this girl, who was in the class above mine) did not know the word for pervert in Japanese—*chikan*—which, if pronounced loudly and clearly enough, causes other riders to look in the direction of that woman agitated enough to raise her voice, and creates enough attention to deter the wandering hands of ordinary men. More often than not, however, a woman molested will endure silently or move away if she can. Not so foreigners, who have trouble keeping their faces immobile and expressionless.

I have heard a few women say they sort of like the attention. So that is lucky for them. But most women are not happy about the situation, and it seems to be growing worse each day. Being the Rider that I am, I have become something of an expert on the subject. The art of train touching, that is.

I have been watching very closely. The train fills up and many people stand packed into the middle spaces between the doors of the car. They hold each other up, face to back, back to back, and side to side. They close their eyes or keep their eyes steady, either not seeing or looking at posters. A few bold riders find space to raise a book to someone's shoulder and read on. A man with his eyes closed moves his hand ever so slightly and waits, moves it more, and waits again. He is from some office, probably, because his briefcase has been wedged next to his legs, and he wears a gray suit with a tie and shiny shoes.

The girl in front of him is wearing a skirt and sweater and jacket and stands with her pocketbook under one arm, her other arm held straight across her breasts and holding on to the pocketbook strap. She feels someone touch her lightly on the buttocks, a slight touch: surely someone is just adjusting his or her position, though she suspects then that it is a man. Unable to move, she breathes with more difficulty, continuing to stare at the fabric in the suit in front of her, a woven tweedy wool of some businessman's overcoat.

Then she feels it again. That touch to the buttocks. In her eyes so steady, in an immobile, seemingly unconcerned face, I watch her comprehend the violation of her body's borders in one lightning quick look of consternation, fear, and disgust. If she turns to look behind her, she sees only the closed eyes of ordinary men in suits.

When she can, she moves out of the train and lets disembarking riders get out, then gets on again, this time near a woman standing next to the silver bar armrest, and hopes that the man in front of her will keep his hands to himself. It seems so common now, three to ten perverts per car in any given minute during rush hour.

The secretaries used to talk about train perverts at lunch. They all brought box lunches to work and spread the contents on the large table in the glassed-in conference area. On the days when I was not lunching with Fukuzawa-san, I lunched with the other women. There were five of us—it was a small trading company—or sometimes six when the secretary from the other office came by.

All of us had, of course, been felt up by some man in the train. I had decreased my own incidences to three per month, since I had worked out a schedule to avoid rush hour; the boss allowed me privileges due to my English ability. He needed me for evening dinners with clients, as the negotiations primarily took place over sake.

At any rate, I can still see Kamo-san's shoulders twitching when we talked about how disgusting it was and which rush trains to absolutely stay away from, and other tips about *chikan.* The problem was not only a question of what to do when we felt molested, but in determining that some man had actually been touching us deliberately. They were very clever, those men— sneaky, even pretending that they were trying to find space for themselves, and touching girls within their reach.

Kamo-san was not by any standards a pretty woman. She was about twenty-nine and lived with her mother, who was ailing in health yet still made her a lunch box—the old-fashioned kind, *o-bentoo*—every day. One day over lunch, Kamo-san told us that she had been followed home the night before. Four of us were sitting around the conference table that day with our food spread all over, the boss out to lunch somewhere.

"I got off my train and changed to a bus and got off where I always do. I wasn't thinking about anything, just walking along for a while, and then I noticed footsteps behind me. It was quite a ways behind me, you know, so I didn't think much about it, but then the steps came closer and closer. Definitely a man's footsteps." She swallowed hard. All of us felt chills. This was not a typical story for the serious Kamo-san to tell.

"I began to get a little scared then because there aren't as many streetlights on the way, so I walked a little faster. But he came closer and closer, and just as I was coming to a streetlight, a man suddenly appeared right in front of me and blocked my way. My heart was going *ga-boom, ga-boom, ga-boom,* and I was shaking in my knees." She shuddered and her eyes grew wide open.

"So I shouted out, 'What are you doing?' I don't know how I said it, I was so frightened, and I thought the words wouldn't come out, but they did. Isn't that a silly thing to say? But he ran away! God, I thought, God, that was lucky. There was a streetlight right there, and I thought, God, what if I hadn't been near that light? . . . God, I was lucky. And I got home as fast as I could, but I was worried that he might have followed or seen where I went. He was a young man, too—not over twenty, I'd guess. What he'd want with me, I don't know."

She took off her glasses, shaking her head from side to side; wiping the lenses clean with a handkerchief, she put them back on and looked around the table.

"It's not as if I look like Mizuno-san. Then he might have a reason." She laughed. "But it was really frightening. I'm afraid to go home after dark anymore."

Mizuno-san tried to shake off the reference to her beauty. She said, "You'd think they'd have more streetlights in your area. It's a residential neighborhood, isn't it?"

And Taito-san, who was older than the rest of us, said very seriously, "It is frightening, isn't it? It never used to be that way. But even I have to be careful of those kinds of men."

"What do you mean, those kinds of men?" Kamo-san said. "This was a young man, you know. And it seems we can't talk about a group of men as being different anymore. I don't think there's such a clear distinction as there was in the past. There only seem to be more and more of them, especially on the trains, and now I have to be careful on my way home in a residential area. It's frightening."

"It does seem to be more and more common," I said. "We've just been luckier than Kamo-san."

As if given license to vent, Kamo-san continued: "I think that they don't go after attractive women so much. They like beautiful women, but they aim for women who are not very pretty because they're . . . perhaps safer or something, if you know what I mean."

"Oh come, Kamo-san, how can you say such a thing like that

about yourself? It just isn't true," said Taito-san. She picked up the kettle and started pouring tea.

"That's right," Mizuno-san chimed in with her sweet voice.

"Absurd," I added. "You were just unlucky is all. Still, you'd better take more care when you're out after dark."

"But it's dark when we leave the office. At least now, in the winter," Kamo-san protested. She looked unconvinced by our performance, and we all knew that we had lied a little for the sake of the group.

Silently, Taito-san poured the tea. She was looking strained of late, and showed her forty-odd years. Her makeup was caking on her chin. All of us knew she was getting ready to say something.

"Can you imagine what it is like for me to stand on a train and feel some man stick his hand on me? I'm not young like you, and when it happens to me I feel more than disgusted. I feel insulted and laughed at, to be touched like that by a man who can tell that I am a single woman—past my chance for marriage. I go home to my apartment where there is no one to talk to and no one to tell how angry I was at some dirty man on the train!" She looked at each of us in turn. "You're lucky to have your mother, Kamo-san, and Mai—you have a husband, of course. Mizuno, you have your friend who rooms with you. I don't know. I suppose we all must put up with living in a city. But I do my best to avoid those men. That's why I don't take the train from this station: I walk to Tokyo Station and wait until I can get a seat, so I don't have to stand in a crowded car. It costs me about a half hour in extra time, but that's the only way I can keep commuting to this office."

"It's harder when you're living alone," Mizuno-san said quietly.

"*Soo desu ne*" (That's true, isn't it?), the rest of us murmured sympathetically.

"I wouldn't have it any other way," Taito-san concluded smoothly. "I can't live with another person. I like my solitude, and

I think that anyone who has lived alone finds the same thing."

"You might be right," I said. "But I think I couldn't do it. If I had my choice, I would live with other people. I think, more than anything else, I'm afraid of being lonely."

"You would think differently," insisted Taito-san.

"I don't know."

"Nor will you," she said.

I didn't answer. It was not worth arguing, particularly since I wasn't sure that Taito-san was wrong. Certainly, at least, I had married with the intention of not living alone.

The subject turned to a phone call for the boss, which Kamo had taken, as we packed up our empty boxes before Fukuzawa-san got back. Mizuno-san said something about wasn't it funny when the boss left the phone off the hook and went to another phone and forgot all about the first call until Taito-san would remind him of it. Whereupon he'd cry, "Oh, no!" and run to the other phone where some client was still waiting on the line, listening to recorded music. It was funny only because he was always doing things like that, yet would deny that he was the absent-minded sort.

I spent the rest of that afternoon dreaming at my desk. Would I like to live alone? It was a good question. I would have liked to go home and stretch out on the floor in front of the TV set, or open a bag of peanuts and raisins, put some Mozart on the stereo, and take an hour-long hot bath with Mozart, the peanuts, and the raisins. . . . Or call up Natsuko and stay on as long as we wished, to talk without Nobu butting in all the time with "But why did she call? Just to talk?" What would I do? God, the list was as infinite as my imagination. . . .

And I really let my imagination overcome me sometimes, especially when I was on the train going home at night after work. My reveries would take me past my normal stop, and follow me as I backtracked, sweeping me along to my door past the vegetables and milk and margarine that I needed in order to make dinner. And I'd have to go back out again or borrow from my neighbor, a good and generous woman who brought over salads and Jell-O when she was interested in knowing how Nobu and I were getting along.

I was glad I worked at an office and didn't have to listen to her drivel about sex all day. When she cornered me on the weekends, she would tell me crude stories that her husband and his friends told over all-night mah-jongg games. She was also quite familiar with sex magazines, and was the only woman I ever met who actually went out and bought men's sex comics—big, lunky books with pink and orange covers and women with grotesquely huge breasts and/or guns coming out of their vaginas. Things like that.

I could borrow food from her if I had to. Or go back to the stores I'd passed so blissfully, dreaming of a white Persian cat— or maybe a small dog—that would greet me at my mahogany door upon my return. Inside there would be a vase on a lovely little table just filled to capacity with chrysanthemums and ferns, and further in was a room with sweet new tatami mats and an alcove made of cherrywood. In the alcove: nothing but a cello, with a bow and a music stand. A few papers would lay artfully scattered about.

The room would look out on a garden, a very private garden with rocks and a stream and no man-carved objects of stone, as there are in so many gardens. I would have only to sit and prepare to play the cello. Perhaps I would need a chair, too, to play.

Pick up the fish, get a couple of carrots, get a jar of coffee. Back to the door, unlock the door, let it bang metallically behind me, remove my shoes, put on slippers—*better throw those out they're way past repair,* dump the groceries in the kitchen, and start the rice. There was dinner to prepare, the plants to water, the bath to run, the records to put away, and the bedroom to sweep.

"If you didn't insist on keeping that job, there wouldn't be any trouble like this!" Nobukazu had found a worm in the spinach that I had washed and boiled and eaten much of already.

"You could stay around here and get to the markets at three or four o'clock like all the other women do. When the fish and the vegetables are fresh! Not like this—from some supermarket where the vegetables sit for days on end! *Iya da yo!*" (Yuck!) He shuddered at the plate still before him. I took it away.

"I don't want to stay home. I like my work. I guess I just wasn't careful enough when I washed that stuff." I was feeling sick to think I had eaten a few of those little white worms myself, and I wondered if I wouldn't get nauseous and throw up. If I did, I'd have to hold my own head because Nobu had such a weak stomach when it came to anything like vomiting or spiders or worms in the spinach. I thought I'd checked the goods over so carefully at that store. I'd never gotten bad vegetables from them before, except for a bunch of cucumbers once—they were hollow inside.

"Besides, we could never afford an apartment like this if I wasn't working. You know that."

"You've reminded me enough, haven't you?" He was getting nasty. "And what about when we have children? Are you going to tell me that you don't want children because of this apartment? You are your father's daughter, I can see. Look at your mother—she never minded that her garden was not wide, or that her mats were a little musty. But you! You have to have new straw and a garden ten times the size of your mother's!"

"And shared by three other apartments as well. You forget that it isn't even our garden here."

"Still, we don't have to have three full rooms and a kitchen. It's a waste of space."

He was getting totally irrational, I thought.

"Two rooms big enough to lay out one bed in each. And the third so large it holds only your desk! You must be crazy. We can't live in anything less," I said.

"We can save money if you stay home," he pressed. "Train passes and all that—they cost. We could buy food that's fresh from the vegetable truck and costs half the price of supermarket food."

"How would you know what the prices in the supermarkets are? How do you know if the truck's prices are cheaper?"

"Natsuko said something about it."

"Natsuko? When did you see Natsuko?"

"I didn't see her, she said it the last time she was over."

"I sure don't remember discussing food with her."

"Well, I know I heard her talk about it. They come to her apartment block and all the ladies buy their food off the truck. It's a lot cheaper." He blushed then; at the time I thought he was just embarrassed to be discussing such matters as vegetable trucks.

"Anyway," he was fairly shouting by now, "you won't have to spend all your money on those skirts you buy in the office from that crook!"

I should have quit right then. But I was so tired of the way he watched me spend my money. And I was a careful spender. I had even started a bank account, thinking ahead to buy a home outside of Tokyo—one with a mahogany door, and a little cat. I had planned to surprise Nobu with my diligent savings.

"He isn't a crook, Nobu. He comes in because he's a friend of Madame Kyoko from the other office. He gives us clothing—beautiful things at half price—only three or four times a year at the most. And even then I rarely buy anything over three thousand yen."

"He comes in on payday, doesn't he? You're going to tell me that Kyoko Fukuzawa isn't in on that business? Six office girls with fat pay envelopes and the Madame standing around? Hah! It's a racket, Mai, and you've fallen for it." He shook his head.

"Perhaps she is in on it. I'd be. It's great business sense when you think about it." It really was very smart of the Madame, and all of us knew she was getting something from it, but since she often bought things for herself when we spread those blouses and skirts and dresses out on the conference table after hours . . . well, you couldn't blame her, and the prices were so good and the quality of the goods so incredibly fine—for the price, that is. And besides, I often thought she was having an affair with that young man who brought the clothes. He was such a flatterer, and he usually insisted on seeing how we looked in the new styles. He never was lewd or peeked into the boss's office where we changed, but sat quietly until we had finished trying on and pawing over the goods. Then he started dickering.

"Those three skirts, no, *four* of those skirts for nine thousand yen."

"He must be crazy!" Kamo-san would whisper in my ear. "That's less than three thousand yen a skirt!"

"But only three of them are taken so far. Mai-san, don't you want to try this one on? You, too, Mizuno-chan, see what this looks like on," Madame would say.

And so we'd all try on more until there was something that fit us, and honestly, they were all very nice things anyway, so it wasn't as if we were being forced to buy something that hung perpetually in a closet somewhere.

But Nobukazu wasn't keen on the idea. I never should have told him, I guess, but I had thought he would be pleased to hear I was saving money on my office wear. Instead, he told me that the three thousand yen which I had just spent could have gone toward "the Baby"—a mythical entity that he decided at one point he wanted more than anything else. More than me, certainly, and perhaps more for his mother than himself.

14 THE STORY OF REIKO AND A LIE TOLD OVER TEA

My sisters, I wanted a baby, of course. But I thought I could have it anytime: it was easy enough to get. And with the money I had saved—partly from my work and partly from our father, who mailed a stipend faithfully to Mama every two months—we could have lived quite comfortably in our apartment and had a baby and fed him. Even if we had a her, it would be okay because we could always make a him: such was my belief at the time.

My mother-in-law wanted a him. She never said so, in so many words, but she did tell me that it was awfully nice to have a boy around, otherwise what would we do in our old age, and not enough money to take care of us? She couldn't stop talking about her life. She herself was very smart to have not one but two boys, she said. See how Nobukazu's older brother takes care of her and her husband, now that both of them are losing their eyesight and their hearing!

Yes, it was marvelous, the way my brother-in-law and sister-in-law took care of the old couple. After Nobu's grandmother passed away—his mother's mother, that is—there was no need to stay on the big estate. It was time to turn to the eldest son. Nobu was still in college at the time, but his brother was a doctor. He and his wife had built up a large practice: there was a clinic out front for emergencies, a surgical area and house for the doctor's family adjacent to that, and, in a separate building at the back of the property, a two-story convalescent hospital—away from the noise of the road. In between the front buildings and the convalescent hospital was a vast garden. And that was where Nobu's brother built a small cottage for his parents. The whole layout looked like this:

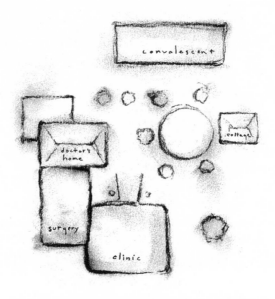

Father and Mother, as I called them then, had all they needed for their retirement. Every morning and every night just before dusk, Father walked around in the garden. He was slow and carried a cane. Mother was much healthier than he. She planted seeds which Nobu bought constantly for her at the department store near his office, or watched television with the old man.

All the young nurses went in to visit during the day for Mother's tea and a shoulder to cry on. Her son (my brother-in-law, the doctor) was too harsh with them, they told her, pouting. He disapproves of every young man they are seen with and complains that all his nurses leave him to get married. Well, and maybe he's right after all the training it takes to work properly with a skilled surgeon, if his nurses and aides leave him high and dry, he has a right to grow bitter. . . . They'd talk on. And at other times he's so sweet, you know, his wife is smart to be working right there with the billing, otherwise. . . . Some of those new ones that come in fresh from nursing school and full of the soap operas, well, it's just a smart thing that the wife's in the office, don't you think so? They'd giggle and calm down a bit.

And Mother would nod her head and pour boiling water from the kettle atop the gas stove into a beautiful little teapot that she had had for years. It was Hagi pottery, with five cups to match. Year after year she listened to the problems of young nurses and laughed at their jokes. It's hard to tell if Father heard them. His hearing was questionable, but he did manage to hear what he wanted to. By and by, one by one, the young nurses *would* leave the practice to get married, saying, "A girl's got a right to happiness, doesn't she?" A few would stay on despite being married, but it seemed eventually they left too because the children need a mother at home, and so forth. Turnover was high. Every time we visited Mother, she had a new tale to tell.

It was a good situation for an older couple like Nobukazu's parents. Naturally, they wanted to see that Nobu and I had the same. "Even if you have three girls," she advised me in her little cabin, "one of them will be smart, a career girl like you. Make sure she becomes a professional, though. She'll be able to take care of you both then, and if she marries, you can take her husband as your son, if you please."

"People don't do that much anymore."

"They don't?" She eyed me. "Of course they do. They can, anyway."

I never argued with her more than a sentence or two. We were not on arguing terms, really, and if I were to challenge her, say, on calling me a career girl while at the same time insisting that I would have children and quit work, we would either end up nowhere or have a terrible fight. Why argue? She was right. I wasn't a career girl. At least I didn't think I was.

"I suppose in another few years I'll be ready, Mother. Don't you worry about it." I smiled.

"A woman can't decide when she is ready, Mai dear. She simply must have children when she can, for if she wonders if she is ready, she will never have them at all." Mother was known for her wise sayings. She continued, "A child would bring joy to your lives. Do you think I haven't noticed? You and Nobu seem to be drifting apart a little, don't you think? What good are old people who just keep getting older? You need children to remind you of youth and bring you new energy."

I kept quiet.

"Haven't you any wish for the companionship of children? Of course, you're working now, but certainly Nobu spends some time away on business and you are left alone at night in a silent apartment. . . ." She seemed to be waiting for an answer.

It was not the first time we had had this conversation. I looked down into my empty teacup, saw the bits of green leaves that sat in a tiny pool in the bottom. Mother went on, gently probing. I knew she was desperately trying to understand my stubbornness, this "Mai" woman who had married her younger son, this woman who was not unreasonable, but perhaps thought too much.

With most women there was no question, no prompting to do: they merrily had their weddings and got pregnant and had babies to bring up. Mai was no different from ordinary women, it seemed to her—Mai promised children to Nobukazu and his parents, and yet, after five years, there they were, she working in an office and he coming home to only his wife. It seemed a shame they were waiting so long. Had they no friends with children? Could they not imagine the sound of high voices squealing and laughing and calling for them?

Mother poured more tea.

"Mai-san, let me tell you a story about a nurse I once knew, many years ago when this place was barely more than a surgical clinic. Now what was her name? Saeko . . . Was it Saeko?" The old woman pressed her eyes shut.

"Not Saeko. She was tall and rather boyish in her build . . . had a lovely smile, and the oddest eyes! Light brown eyes like the color of barley tea . . . Reiko! That's it. Reiko-san. A girl from the town." The wrinkled eyelids opened slowly. Mother settled back on her heels, sitting *seza*, Japanese-style, to tell the story of Reiko.

"Some years ago, Mai, there was a nurse whom my son hired to be his surgical assistant. He wanted someone with steady hands, someone who not only had the nerve to stand next to him through all emergency cases but someone so competent she could practically handle the operation herself. Naturally, when Reiko showed up pretty and fresh from nursing school, and a town girl at that, he was skeptical of her.

"But she was built something like a man—strong, wide back, and sturdy broad shoulders. I guess she played sports at one time, perhaps volleyball or swimming when she was in school. She had excellent recommendations from her instructors. And she was a capable and brave person, never flinched at the doctor's tirades, and never indicated the slightest repulsion at the sight of blood. It was not long before she became the doctor's right-hand aide. In her spare time, she visited Father and me. We'd have a cup of tea, eat some rice crackers, talk about the doctor and his many moods— his utter compassion for each and every patient that walked through his door, and his absolute intolerance of frivolity from his staff. In those days, none of his staff was ever to leave him, he said, or even daydream about the idea." Mother smiled at the memory.

"My son was of the opinion that this was a clinic, and this was medicine, and heartbreak was intolerable in a place where it was hard enough to keep patients' hearts beating. Once in a while I'd go to him myself, and I'd tell him, Now listen, son, you are a respected doctor with a small, growing practice and a top-notch staff. If you had any brains, you'd mention to Miss Reiko that her eyes are red and swollen and she'd better get a bit of sleep instead of sweeping the entrance hall and washing the instruments after hours. What about her eyes? he'd ask. Miss Reiko? Why, she's fine, Mother, there's nothing wrong with her. And besides, a good nurse should take great pride in caring for the surgical instruments. She's not a maid, of course, but I see nothing wrong with having her clean around a bit.

"But the entrance hall, I'd press him. And haven't I seen her doing some records at the desk? Oh, he'd say, I hadn't noticed. And off he'd go, as if he was thinking of something important that just then struck him. And before you knew it, Reiko-san would be taking a few days' vacation with her family while the doctor paced around, hoping she would get back before there was a serious accident or something. He really depended on that woman."

The old woman paused and smoothed her cheek with one hand, rubbing the skin rhythmically.

"Things went on this way for some three years or thereabouts, and Reiko showed no intention of leaving or getting married or anything, and everyone privately said what a stroke of luck it was for the doctor to find such a solid career nurse so early in his practice and all.

"Well, I am a skeptical woman and pretty experienced about the world, and so I thought it would be wise if I asked her about her plans. You know, what did her parents want her to do, did they want her to have an arranged marriage or were they content to have her be an old maid and settle into the hospital as her career? All this I decided I would find out from Reiko one day—not asking point-blank, exactly, but in as confidential a way as I could. Though she had never been secretive with me, don't you think it odd, Mai-san, that she never talked to me about the kind of husband she'd like to have, or where she'd like to have her house?

"I waited for a good chance, which came when my first grandchild was born—your niece, Masako. Reiko had said to me, 'Well, the doc's got himself a little girl. Wonder if the tyke knows she's going to be a doctor?' and she laughed hilariously. I laughed, too, but I was taken aback. My granddaughter a doctor? Surely Reiko had a strange sense of humor! But then she said to me, 'You know, the doctor is no ordinary man. He actually did tell me that he didn't care what it was, it was going to be a doctor of some kind—most likely a surgeon. Otherwise, how else can he get himself an apprentice who will stick around as long as he's alive to carry on with his hospital? He says this hospital will be five stories high someday, and with convalescent quarters over here in the back of the garden. He says it will take all of his daughters and sons to staff this place. How large a staff do you and your wife plan to produce? I asked him as a joke, but he was not amused at all. I've never seen him so sober, so absorbed in thought. I think it must have been that patient this morning that affected him like that—an accident victim it was, early today. Came in by ambulance. He didn't even have a chance, though. Hit on a bike.' Reiko shook her head.

"I asked Reiko how old the victim was. 'Thirty-two,' she answered. 'Married, two kids.' Then the nurse turned her head away. Why, she was crying! I went and refilled the teakettle. The morning's work must have been quite an ordeal, I thought to myself. Reiko, of all of them, was the strongest: cool and efficient, never involved, ever the professional assistant. She was the one who told the families the bad news first; then the doctor would speak to them, and leave them for Reiko—she treated them for shock, when it was called for. Held grown men down while another nurse administered sedatives.

"I poured her a cup of tea and waited until her shoulders stopped heaving and her crying turned to a quiet sobbing. 'Reiko, what is it?' I asked her. 'Was it someone you knew?' No, she shook her head. She said, 'Oh, it's just that he was so young, and his wife—she couldn't have been over twenty-five. She looked destroyed, you know, and the children were so serious and scared. I couldn't help but think that it could have happened to anyone.'

" 'To anyone?' I said to Reiko. 'You're talking about the wife, right? You mean it could have happened to you, Reiko.' "

Mother stopped to cough, and sipped some tea. I kept quiet.

"So she began crying all over again, but this time she was so loud I had to close the door to the cabin—that's how much pain she had locked inside herself; it made an awful noise coming out all at once like that. When she stopped crying, she told me she never wanted children, never wanted to get married and live with a man who may or may not be home at night, and she wasn't stupid, why were her parents always pressing her to get married and have children when they know damn well that no man would spend the time to know her children anyway?

"Did it really matter that a father died on a bicycle today, leaving two little children? Financially, yes, there was a big difference. But, chances were, she told me, he was just an ordinary man who spent his money on drink, and his Sundays playing catch with the boy, and on Mondays he went to the bars—in the name of business, of course. In time there would be a mistress who would hold his true affections, and wasn't it just as well for the young wife that he died now before he became like all the rest? Wasn't it better for a woman to suffer a tragic separation by death than the emotional pain coming later after years of alienation from her husband?

"Incredible. I was impressed that she got it all out, anyway. And I asked, 'How is it you've come to think this way? Perhaps you've carried this with you from another life. Not all men are cold strangers to their children and their wives, Rei-chan, and not all men have second wives. Why, look at the doctor!' But Reiko sat with her mouth set in a line and her eyes downward. She breathed deeply. Then, speaking slowly, like she had to teach me something—me, an old woman!—she said, 'Many, many men have mistresses and bargirls whom they see quite regularly. The only difference between the past and today is that nowadays women are divorcing faster and more often. The truth is young wives don't want to be second anymore. I know I don't need the kind of life my friends have in their marriages.'

"Reiko told me, 'At the wedding receptions of each and every one of my girlfriends—girls from around here—the sake flowed and the guests all got drunk and the speeches got longer and longer. And when it came time for the groom's buddies to speak, they each got up and said how rowdy the groom had been in his college days and they'd turn to the bride and say, Please, let my old buddy out of the house once in a while so we can go drinking and play mah-jongg, just for old times' sake, please? Always there was some clown in the gang who got down on his knees in front of the bride then, and everybody laughed and laughed, and they flattered the bride, and—Boom!—sent the happy couple away and off on their honeymoon.

" 'But where do you suppose that husband is months later? Back to his once-a-week games with the boys, and out drinking on business two nights a week, and the other nights he gets home at nine P.M. for bath, dinner, TV, and bed. Then it's up by six and off. Not for me, that kind of life. It would take a most unusual man and most unusual circumstances for me to marry!'

"All this Reiko said to me with great emotion—and yet she was extremely clear. I said to her, 'Who says you have to marry a salaryman?' 'My parents,' she answered. 'They want someone who has a steady position in the company, someone who gets benefits the older he gets. Not like a schoolteacher, who makes such a low salary. As a couple, we have to be able to give some money to my parents as well as have children. What better person than a company man? Of course, being that I'm a nurse, a doctor would be ideal for me, but . . .'

"Well, right then, Mai, she blushed a deep red. I was not sure why at first—the only thing I could think of was that her family was not of any status to speak of and I had embarrassed her by pushing too hard about these questions of marriage and so forth. But when I thought it over later, it was she who had volunteered all this information. She needed to share it with someone. Possibly she felt guilty about being so selfish—to disobey her parents' wishes when in a few years' time, they would need to lean on her. But she was so certain that she was right, and that marriage could only bring her pain. And in the meantime, the way things were going, there was every indication that if she stayed at the hospital, her salary might rise substantially over time—especially once she turned thirty, when there would be very little danger of her running off to get married. In which case, she could afford to support her parents in their old age. Actually, I am sure that she fully intended to do that—except for one thing that she had not accounted for.

"She had fallen in love with my son. She realized it in that very split-second moment when she dreamed aloud to me that she would like to have a doctor as a husband. She realized her love then, and she realized the gravity of the situation she had found herself in. In less than two months, Mai, she was gone. Married, by arrangement, to a man none of us knew. And as none of us attended the wedding, we only found out by hearsay that he was with a chemical firm in Osaka, and that they would live there.

"It was a long time before the doctor got over that one. Of course, since that time he has never expected to keep his nurses. He'll growl at them and lecture them about their boyfriends, but he never seems surprised when they say they're leaving. As a matter of fact, even Tanaka-san, who's about thirty-five, you know, complains to me that he teases her a little bit too much about when she's leaving him to go on her honeymoon."

Mother smiled, satisfied, and rubbed the edge of the quilt of the *kotatsu* heater. I wondered what she wanted to know from me. And I did not have to wait long.

"Mai-san, sometimes we become close with men in our workplace. It can make a woman forget her priorities in life."

So that was it—Mother thought I might be in love with Fukuzawa-san! That I saw Nobu as a typical salaryman, an ordinary man, who would fool around on me. That I was afraid to have children because I was so insecure. . . . She and I were truly facing a culture gap here. And, once again, I was in no position to fight. As I said earlier, we were not on arguing terms. But this baby thing was getting out of hand. Suppose she hinted to Nobu that I was growing sweet on my boss!

I watched Mother's hand tracing the bunting on the blanket, an old woman obsessed with her mothering and her grandmothering, not willing to let anyone stand in her way. All things considered, she was really very healthy for an old woman. I wondered if Father had had a mistress. I was pretty sure he had at one time devoted himself to a woman in the next city over. Nobu had mentioned it once, but said that he himself was not positive. Still, no matter what, this was a powerful woman I was facing.

"Mother, if I tell you this, you won't tell Nobu, will you?"

"Of course not, Mai, we're speaking woman to woman now."

"I can't ever have children," I blurted out, and real tears came popping out of the corners of my eyes. To my own surprise, once I had said those words aloud, I began to feel incredibly sad, overwhelmingly depressed. I was thinking about how sad Reiko's story was, in addition to my own story.

"I've been seeing a specialist in Tokyo, and unless there's some kind of miracle, I may not ever get pregnant. I'm sorry, Mother. I just couldn't bring myself to tell Nobu yet. I can't tell anybody yet, and I don't want anybody to know. Not even my closest friend knows. I can't talk to her because I'm so jealous that she has a baby already. I just need more time."

"There, there. Oh, Mai-chan, I'm sorry. I'm so sorry," Mother said, handing me tissues as I wept. Then she sat back and pulled out a handkerchief stuffed in the sleeve of her kimono. She dabbed at her own eyes.

I knew she would tell Nobu that same day if she could. She was that kind of person. I counted on it. And I was right. From that day forward, no one bothered me about having babies anymore. The trade-off was that I had to sit on the outermost edges of Nobu's family circle, not quite tossed into the cold but not quite warm, either. Things were never the same.

It was a stupid lie, I suppose, but the only self-defense I could think of at the time. I convinced myself that it would all be okay anyway, because when I did finally allow myself to get pregnant, I could make up a miracle operation—tell them all that new laser techniques had cleared my tubes from being blocked, or something like that.

I counted on my own resourcefulness. I had never been let

down by my resourcefulness. But I never once considered that my words would get to Natsuko's ears, or that they would have such disastrous effects on my marriage, on Nobu, on Natsuko, on Natsuko's decision to bear a second child, on Tomio's reaction, on Mother's reaction . . . and on and on. It had seemed innocent enough at the time we were drinking tea, there in the garden. It felt like a thousand years ago.

15   BAGWOMEN I HAVE KNOWN

Young girl, thirteen, jeans, bandanna scarf, platform boots, short jacket, and a bag with a picture of a sweet-looking kitten with red ribbon and blue skies. The train was filled in the late afternoon with bags and bag carriers. Many were matching. As for myself: brown coat, brown boots, rust-colored scarf, brown shopping bag.

So many bag slogans in English or French these days. Bags without slogans are designer creations: plaid, Snoopy, flowers, old cars.

There are, around town, women who carry shopping bags. Whatever they have with them, whatever they buy along the way gets a place in the bag and is rarely seen by other riders. I imagine there are lunches of rice balls wrapped in seaweed and shoes and cosmetics and magazines hidden in those bags. If I were a train conductor, I would peek into all the bags that are abandoned on the train and delight in their contents.

Or perhaps I wouldn't.

One day some years ago, my boss told me that he had lost his umbrella on a train at Ueno Station, a black umbrella with a carved wooden handle, and not because he had such great attachment to his possessions or anything, but thinking it was an unusually good umbrella—"very functional," as he was fond of saying—he went to the Ueno Station Lost and Found to retrieve it. Whereupon the conductor chuckled, took out a key from a locked drawer, and led him to a very large room underground. It had one wall lined with black umbrellas, just thousands of them, many with carved wooden handles but not one appearing exactly like the one he'd lost. Soon he began to forget what that umbrella had looked like. Interspersed among the black ones were hundreds of clear plastic, plaid-patterned, checked, blue, green, gold, red, amber, purple, and white umbrellas, designer umbrellas with the signatures of Nina Ricci, Yves St. Laurent, and Ungaro, and Walt Disney umbrellas, cartoon characters, butterflies, and more.

Recovering from his initial confusion, Fukuzawa-san walked over to where the bulk of the black umbrellas nested against each other. He continued to walk past plastic handles, rusty handles, handles with long crooknecks and short crooknecks, handles that looked like hammer heads, and handles that were carved from wood and shellacked. At last he chose a sturdy-looking, carved, wooden-handled, easy-open umbrella and exclaimed, "Oh, yes! This seems to be it!"

As he followed the sniggering conductor out of the room, he let his eyes roam over the hundreds of bags and packages wrapped in large *furoshiki* cloths, many of them sitting on tables, and all of them apparently left untampered with. If not one of those bags and parcels has been opened, he thought, there must be a virtual ton of petrified baked goods and moldy sneakers and rotting pickles.

The thought made him slightly nauseous. But, as he told me, since he was a very "thorough thinker," he began to consider that in those wedding *furoshiki* cloths and certainly in some of those very full and refined-looking shopping bags from prestigious department stores, there must be an equal number of treasures—real loot! New blouses! Silk scarves! Stockings, gloves, and slippers! A dainty little change purse, a pearl ring, perfume sachets, wristwatches, and tortoise-shell hairpieces. Neckties, Italian shoes, soap. Books of all kinds, works of art, handicrafts, china dolls, and baskets of all shapes and sizes. Sex toys, rice cookers, calculators . . . All that new merchandise sitting wasted in the Lost and Found at Ueno Station.

He devised a plan to get the bags. After all, it was simple enough for him to walk in and say, "This is my umbrella," he thought, and the station workers had one less umbrella on their hands and he had himself a new umbrella and everyone was happy, were they not? He confided in me a wild plan. If a corps of women were to "work" the Lost and Found departments of all the major stations in Tokyo—claiming bags, that is—he could sell the watches and other precious new merchandise in Ameyoko, where the Hong Kong smugglers go to dump jewelry, and the women would get a nice cut plus something from their bags, something they had a particular hankering for. What could be easier? Would I join his corps of Lost Bagwomen?

Not that I ever entertained the idea. But you can't help thinking about those things. Imagining yourself doing such things. It was ludicrous. I was squeamish to the extreme about rotting foods and strange odors that issue forth from other people's bags, even though I now know that the station workers are responsible for opening and disposing of bags that contain offensive odors. I know this from a newspaper that was left behind on the upper rack of a late-night train. The stench of one problem bag, said an article in that paper, was powerfully foul—so putrid and searing to the nostrils that the young worker assigned to take care of the bag began vomiting just prior to the unveiling, at which time his superior stepped in and found, to his great disgust and greater dismay, a fully formed baby with a plastic bag over its little head.

And so, although the risks were minimal, I refused the boss's criminal scheme and continued my office job. I am much too shy for such shystering anyway, I thought. If a poor station worker has so much respect for property, why, then, I should too.

But, as I said, abandoned bags are simply not opened or confiscated: they hold both treasures and ordinary things, concealing, containing all the things that Shoppingbagwomen have to carry.

I love bags. Bags and their carriers are best viewed in the train in the off-hours. If they are crowded into a train during rush hour, you can't read them so well: often bags get pushed to one side, are folded over and held close to the chest. Or else they're crushed between the outer thigh of the Shoppingbagwoman and the thigh of a stranger. They also tend to be dominated by the rush-hour briefcases, heavy, black, slender cases that take priority in the racks above people's heads.

My mother used to be a Shoppingbagwoman. She had a blue bag that came from America, which said DUTY-FREE SHOPPER on it, with a little airplane in the corner and a phone number scribbled in blue ink close to the handles. She took it with her whenever she went "into town"—center city Tokyo, that is. She went every three months or so, never alone but always with her sister, my cousins, and me. Often there was a box of chocolate-covered pretzels or bean-paste patties in the bag, which she doled out to my cousins and me, one for each and not another till we'd gone three stops. "Hurry, train, hurry!" my littlest cousin Izumi sang out, and we turned it into a drawn-out chant just enjoying the words, looking and laughing at each other. Louder and louder we sang, "Hurry, train, hurr-rr-rry!" till finally we were hushed by Auntie, who said that she had heard of little girls whose behavior so shocked the riders on one train, one fine day in Tokyo, that they went home and told their families that girls from the countryside had turned their train car into a raucous howl, and weren't those country girls better off at home, tending the chickens? We quieted up seriously, for a minute or two, anyway.

I remember being surprised to think we were bad. Had we been shouting that loudly? It must have been very loud for my sweet Auntie to speak up. Aunt Kaoru was the loveliest person in the world. She still may be, for all I know. She and her family moved away, off to an island where Uncle Taro came from, after his tailor's shop closed down in Yokosuka, where the U.S. Navy base was located. "That's what happens when you work in a military base town," said my mother to me afterwards. "There's a war, there's business. The war winds down, go home." In Uncle Taro's case, the Vietnam War had provided him with plenty of work, what with all those GI's on shore leave. R&R's, they called it. More than my cousins, and much more than Uncle, I missed Auntie. I have not seen Auntie now for ten years.

The bag I have been carrying is a small shopping bag. It is as dark as my coat. It seems natural to carry a bag. I carried first a bookbag to school, and then later, when I was working, I carried a bag to the office since I was always posting packages to foreign countries. The office bag had signs of the Western Zodiac in a big circle in different colors. Eventually, it split along the side and was replaced by a black bag with silver letters that read ROMAN WEATHER REPORT with the average temperatures in Rome beneath.

Ah, but there are some great bags.

I am thinking of the bag in front of me this very afternoon. It said: WE ARE BEAUTIFUL PEOPLE FROM AN UNKNOWN CULTURE, and its bearer was a lonely-looking matron of trim Western dress and some forty years. She looked out into the crowded train, her eyes troubled and brows knitted together. It must have been raining outside: coats were wet, and the crowd was sort of a miserable, subdued crowd.

There must have been at least twenty bagwomen in just my car alone, no doubt due in part to the holidays approaching, which seemed to have sent everyone scurrying for expensive presents to give to relatives, bosses, tutors, and go-betweens who arranged the marriages of daughters and sons. My eyes found a "Ginza Red" bag; John Lennon in photo negative; Isetan Department Store; a bag that said, LETS SPORTS VIOLENT ALL DAY LONG; Kanebo Cosmetics; Marilyn Monroe winking; and a bag that read, WISH IN TWILIGHT over a Hawaiian beach with palm trees, sand, dusk, and lovers holding hands as they stroll along the water's edge.

The beautiful woman from an unknown culture studied the posters hanging in the center aisles. She looked down at her hands next, then at the bag they clutched, then up again sideways, and finally—through a space between the fat man and the tall college boy with the long striped scarf—she peered into a small corner of the window opposite her. With one hand she smoothed the hair over her ears and turned ever so slightly to view the thick chignon at the nape of her neck. It was gloriously lustrous hair, so black it appeared blue. Still, the worried look in her eyes. Turning her head back, she gave a quick glance to the side to see if anyone had been watching her. The fat man, who actually had been watching her the whole time, lifted his eyes and looked out another window.

My mother has blue-black hair like that, and dresses it the same way, though that is not why I have come to think of her now. There was something much less tangible about the similarity between this bagwoman and my mother: they were not alike in the way they dressed, as my mother nearly always wore kimono after she was forty; and certainly my mother never used a train window to adjust her hair or her expression.

Perhaps it was the hair itself: the time and care it takes to dress such voluminous hair every morning—no matter how troubled or tired they feel, no matter how little they smile these days. There is something very resigned in the long combing and pinning, something like the faces of old women who get on the train and just sit with their faces totally devoid of expression, hands folded over handbags, and paying so little attention to the bright posters and swaying of the train. They enter the trains without relief and leave the same way, just stepping out carefully and heading for the elevators as if they had never been in the train at all.

Suddenly I remember a time with my mother in a huge old kitchen with cold stone floors, in the home of my great-uncle, who was a priest. We went there quite often after my dad left us. Mama and Aunt Kaoru and two other women, who I imagine were part-time help, were washing dishes and chopping scallions and so forth. I remember Aunt Kaoru holding a big square of soft white bean curd in one hand, flat on her palm, as she cut it into tiny cubes for the soup. The smell of a low, open smoky fire mingled with the steaming vat of miso soup above it. I sat on the step separating the deep kitchen from the rest of the house, dangling my feet, enjoying all the bustle, and listening to their laughter.

My aunt was making everybody laugh by using men's words and coarse men's language—Mama was laughing so hard she had tears in her eyes, and every time she tried to talk, she couldn't. Of course the more Mama laughed, the more Aunt Kaoru would say. Though I didn't understand the dialect too well, I laughed too because it was just so funny. Auntie was really a clown, and there were merry times in that country kitchen.

When my mother finally caught her breath and attained some sobriety, she scolded her sister for using such words in front of a child who picked up words so easily, adding, "What would the neighbors say, or her teachers for that matter, if she came back to Tokyo talking like that?" Well, that made matters worse and they all ended up laughing again just thinking about Mama's sophisticated Edo neighbors being sworn at by a "little girl with a country mouth."

Those were good times for me, then. And, as things go, that too has changed. My great-uncle died suddenly of stomach cancer, and although my great-aunt struggled for a while at the old house, she showed up in Tokyo one day, frail and shaking, after riding the trains for some three or four hours, all by herself. Exhausted, she slept in my room. Mama, who was anxious and trying hard not to show it, got on the phone to Kaoru right away. Aunt Kaoru showed up within the hour, and she and Mama whispered together and made tea for each other till Great-Aunt woke up.

They held a conference that evening. It was just three ladies and me at the conference. Though they clearly did not ask me to talk, I was allowed to listen, since my father was gone, and since I was ten and should now take part in family events. I will never forget how we drank *bancha* poured from the same teapot, how we decided that it would be better to turn the old estate over to the temple, and how we cried about the whole thing. We put out an extra futon for Aunt Kaoru once she had called Uncle Taro and checked on my cousins. Uncle Taro said he was doing okay but she better come home right away in the morning. Great-Aunt went with Auntie to live, since Mama was working at the dress shop and couldn't take care of her properly during the day.

I never saw my great-aunt again. The funeral was held in the same house she had lived in, now permanently part of the temple grounds, and I have never set foot in that house since.

16 | No Stars

It had been a day for reverie, and sleep. Evening was evident as I awakened from a doze.

Near the doors three men rowdied about together, punching each other and teasing each other as men do, about who paid the bill at the restaurant that night. "Hey, I paid the last time—and the time before that!" laughed one. "Yeah, but we ate cheap *yakitori* at some little dive," called another, hitting the other on the shoulder. "Oh, yeah? A little dive, huh? You sure ate like a horse that time! Hey, Tenma! Doesn't your name mean 'Heavenly Horse,' anyway?" The three roared together happily.

They smelled of warm, savory food, and their faces were flushed with alcohol. I got to thinking about Bunkyo ward. About Kimiko, and pork cutlets, happy groups of men eating, and boiling hot green tea. It had been a year since I had gone there, I realized. Exactly a year ago, just before the holidays.

It meant leaving the train, but that was all right. I wanted to see if it was still raining.

When I got off the train that took me to Bunkyo, a miracle happened.

Lo and behold, the very Stationwoman I had drawn a picture of was stretched out underneath the concrete steps of the platform. She was dead asleep, half-covered by cardboard boxes that had been opened out to form a shelter. Though her body was carrying more layers of cloth, her face looked gaunt and blackened by station dirt. So, she has been living here for at least a year, I thought. I walked on, up the stairs, out into a steady rain.

The pork place was closed. Not only closed but boarded up, with signs that said: RENTAL OPPORTUNITY: CALL RYOTA AGENCY, PLEASE. The rain drove in great sheets now, and I hurried to hide my bag under my coat. Suddenly I was overcome by a feeling of having been there before, standing at the boarded-up restaurant, hiding my bag under my coat the way I had just done. Something caused me to look upstairs to the windows. Was that Kimiko walking behind those drapes? I thought it was a woman. It moved like a woman.

I shook the feeling of déjà vu. Felt the rumble of the subway calling me. But I was not ready to go back. First, I had to find something to eat. It should be something the Stationwoman can eat too, I decided. At a late-night grocery store I picked up hot *manju* dumplings from a revolving glass case. They were cheap and tasty. I ate half of the bean variety and half of the meat ones, then carefully folded the wrapper back over the rest, saving them. The shopkeeper watched me.

"They're for someone else. A poor stationwoman," I told her.

"Ah."

It was a fairly simple thing to leave the bag of still-warm *manju* next to the sleeping woman. She smelled badly, though, so I did not linger by her side. Several late-night riders joined me on the platform, wet, and shaking their umbrellas in every direction. I was glad of their company. The death of Kimiko's restaurant had begun to wear through. I needed to hear the low chatter of friends talking to friends.

I was riding on, feeling the night grow deeper, even though this is a place where the sun never shines, has never shone. Deeper and deeper into the night the train rolled on, the names of each stop so familiar to me I hear them echoing in my head twice, three times before they are announced over the loudspeaker.

If I get back to Rose Maison before midnight, I thought, I could see Emiko again. She might be huddled in the corner again, or perhaps she would have thought to carry an umbrella.

Decided.

I transferred to the line that would take me back home. But despite the comfort of the train, boisterous riders were louder than usual tonight; I had a roaring in my head that propelled me from one car to the next. It was not simply that I was unable to sit still, but that I could not seem to get off the train fast enough.

Passing from car to car, Natsuko seems to be walking behind me. I hold the door for her, and now we are choosing seats. She wants to sit near cute guys. I keep marching on through the train, and she follows, laughing, calling me chicken, singing a song we both got crazy over. "You Better Shop Around," she sings as I hold yet another metal door open for us. She passes through first, wiggling and dancing, and I join in, and we are both singing and dancing the rhythm and blues. . . . Everyone is watching us, but we like that, and we just don't care what anybody thinks anymore. . . . When I get to the end of the line, she is gone.

Up ahead at the top of the stairs there was a black night. I saw no stars. It was not raining, but the cloud cover was heavy. Hurrying, I entered the street half-breathing, daring to hope there was a little hump there, waiting for her mother.

It was too late for a child to be out. . . . *Or is it? Who is Mai to say what should be? Who is Mai to hope for anything?* Angry with the invasion of these thoughts, I concentrated on finding my key.

A small figure was swinging her feet off the low ledge.

Emiko! Joy welled up.

"Komban wa."

"Komban wa," said the little voice. It was young in age but strong and clear, as I remembered it from the previous evening.

"No stars tonight, huh?" I said.

"Nope."

Emiko kept her eyes on the street, looking.

"Waiting for your mommy?"

"Yup."

"Are you sure you want to be sitting there? It looks wet." Rain has soaked the entire ledge.

"It's okay. I've got a sheet of plastic under me. Found it in the trash," she said.

"Oh."

She did not seem to want me there, would not look at me. I felt sure she recognized me from the night before.

"Do you remember talking to me last night—when it was snowing out here?"

"Yup." Still she would not look. I guessed she was scared to talk to a stranger. I guessed maybe she had told her mama that a strangerwoman had been talking to her.

"Well, I'll just be going in now. Good night, Emiko." I turned to let myself in the apartment house.

"Hey," called the little voice. "Want to see what I found?"

I looked back. Emiko reached inside her coat and produced two bears, a mother and a cub. They were the Hokkaido bears I left on the ground next to the trash receptacle that morning when I left for the subway. Seeing them turned my stomach in a queer way. They reminded me of Nobu and the vacation we took years ago, when we were still in love.

"What do you know?" I said. I forced myself to say this as if I was admiring them.

"I like the way the circles of the wood go round and round and round without a stop," said Emiko. She pointed the circles out to me, and I came closer to see. They were pretty.

"Nice." I peered down the street. It was quiet. Only a taxi cruised by from the wrong direction. And a woman with an umbrella clicked up the sidewalk on the opposite side. Two men with briefcases walked ahead of her, also on their way home. I had seen them all on the train.

Emiko asked, "Do you think I can keep them? They were near the trash."

"By all means, you should give those a home," I assured her. Somehow I could not bring myself to tell her the whole truth. It would never do to tell her that I had owned them myself. I felt I had intruded enough already, that if her mother were to find out, she would want to meet me—or worse, give me something in return. I did not want that.

She held them so gently. . . .

"I tell you what, Emiko. I'll do like I did last time. I'll wait until she comes, right here in this shadow. If you want, we can keep on talking that way."

Emiko put the bears back in her coat against her chest, and resumed her vigil. We talked just a few minutes more about why there were no stars, and what if the stars just disappeared altogether one day. Once again, exactly as it had occurred the night before, a long foreign car pulled up, and a woman waved goodbye gaily to the driver, and she walked off with Emiko skipping next to her.

The child was eager to show off her newfound treasures, no doubt.

17   Exposed

I dreamed I was walking down the stairs and somehow it was night—though it must have been morning because it felt like morning. The corridor was dark and long. I rounded a corner and found myself approaching the wickets. A ticket-taker had his back toward me, waiting to take the tickets of passengers who were just getting off the train. They were coming toward me, first only a few in the distance, and then more and more men, businessmen in morning suits with fresh collars. As soon as I could see the details in their clothing, I realized that I had no shirt on; my breasts were bare and exposed. I panicked. Where could I go? I could go back up the stairs, but I could hear more of them coming behind me, crowds on their way to work.

I covered my breasts by folding my arms across my chest, and looked for newspapers in the garbage bin, something to cover myself with. But there were no papers yet—it was too early. I could go to the bathroom. Yes! To the women's bathroom. But God, where was it? How could I not know? I had been here many times before; I knew this station well. I ran back and forth trying to find it, and the people trooped closer and closer and closer and closer. . . .

And suddenly I was in a field, like a golf course on a bright day, and I still had no clothes on top. There were only a few people around, far in the distance. I found a towel and covered myself, holding it calmly in front of me, and when a man approached, I laughed blithely, as though I were just a sunbather. He was a teacher or something, I felt, and he passed me easily with a smile. I ran and ran across the field. Trees gave great shade, and there were many people up ahead. I ran toward them but woke up before I saw their faces.

It was still dark. I was sweating terribly under the electric blanket. I turned it off and lay still. My biology teacher had said that people were mostly water; it's no wonder we wet our beds. A language teacher replied, "Ah, we are such stuff as dreams are made on."

"Made of water, made by dreams. No wonder we wake up sweaty when we dream," I contributed.

It seemed too early to get up, but the bed was damp, so I headed for the bathroom. It was freezing in there. I turned on a little heater next to the toilet. It began to glow in coils of orange, around and around. Like the inside of a toaster, I thought. Big toast on the toilet, I was. Like one of those big pieces you get in coffee shops, with the crust cut off.

Where does the crust go? Who eats it?

I imagined a Chef's Special: Piled Choice Crusts, cut in perfect empty squares, absolutely without a break in their perimeter. Served with chocolate sauce.

I ate tea and toast at the kitchen counter, satisfied I had no plates left for the toast to sit on. I had been trying to get rid of those plates for a long time: it had taken me several weeks to clear them all out of the kitchen, first the Western ones, then all the smaller, Japanese porcelain pieces.

In the bedroom, I stood my *futon* up sideways, and pulled on long stockings. My coat with the hood hung in a dark clump from a hook. Getting light outside already. Funny. It always was light; I have moved, not the sun. The moon moves with me, and we face the sun in the morning. We are now facing the sun. When the sun is out of sight, I'll be home as usual. A little on the late side, in all probability.

The living room was the quietest room in the apartment. I could not pass through it without the same thought always: *Ugly goddamn green curtains and green pillows.* I told the woman I didn't want the curtains, but she never really heard me or something. If only I had said to her, "I don't like your ugly curtains, so push them at some other customer's face but not mine. The curtains are not going to fit."

"They'll fit perfectly," said she. "Goes well with brown. Your table is brown, isn't it?"

How the hell do you know what color my table is, and do you know what color toothbrush I use, too? God, these salespeople really know their stuff. That I can be fooled by this . . .

"Yes, you're right, those are precisely what I had in mind when I came in. Moreover, my table is brown." That's what I told the saleswoman who sold me those green curtains and the *zabuton* pillows to match. My mother-in-law had been with me, standing by, nodding and nodding. The most beautiful things, our Buddhist altar and a cherrywood music box, and the Hakata dolls with their painted faces were all taken by her when she heard our nuptials had de-nupted. So how did I end up with these ugly curtains? And those pillows?

I put on my brown coat and turned off the heater in the bathroom. In the medicine cabinet were three 5,000-yen notes. I took them all, stuffed them in my bag. On the way to the front door I picked up two of the pillows. They stank horribly. You are not supposed to leave pillows in a dark apartment. Mold grew blue-green on the underside. It didn't look bad, oddly.

The pillows fit neatly on top of the garbage-pail lid outside. Better here than in the living room, I thought. Feeling in very good spirits, I headed for the station. The air was several degrees warmer outside than it had been in Rose Maison. Going to be a nice day for the people outside.

An old, bent woman came by pushing a baby carriage full of yogurt milks and coffee milks. She had a cotton scarf wrapped entirely around her mouth and neck. There was a big tie in the back and the fringe trailed over her shoulders. I knew I was early when I saw her. She seemed to nod at me.

Are you nodding or just hunching? Or both, perhaps? Because I've been nodding myself, you know, and wondered if perhaps you had seen me at all?

It's hard to tell in this light. It's early for these eyes. She hunched on. It's hard to tell, an old woman like me, are my friends still nodding to me? My eyes aren't sharp, but I know my coffee milk because it's brown, see? The yogurt milk is yellow. She lifted first brown then yellow.

Why does it hurt me to see you hunched over like that? My back is hurting me, I say to her, without speaking the words aloud.

Then you are young, much, much younger than I, she says back, though your voice is deep. I feel no pain, it hurts me to stand straight, not like you who think it hurts you to see me. Besides, if I don't recognize my friends and they are nodding to me, they are never offended as I appear to be perpetually bowing. She muffled her face up and pushed on down the opposite side of the street.

I hurried down the long concrete walk. The Route 60 gang had written their name all over the walls overnight with white paint. A pail of water stood on a step nearby. I felt my dream again strongly.

It was not unusual for me to dream about having my clothes off. But it had been a long time since I had had one so frightening. In one before this, I dreamed that I was bare-assed and at a party—a wedding party, I think—and before I had a chance to panic and look for clothes, it turned out that I was at a very sexy party, and that everybody was nude and going from room to room and floor to floor in a big house with narrow passageways. I remember looking at everyone quite thoroughly and walking around alone most of the time, exchanging greetings and watching all the activity.

Sometimes I imagine that everyone in the train has their clothes off. I tried it today: that woman in the plaid coat with the big gold earrings has medium-round breasts that are sagging along with the corners of her mouth. Those two men laughing and joking with those coy office girls have little boys' penises and they compared them in the shower when they were in high school gym. The old man with his eyes closed has a tremendous whanger, but he can never find a tailor quite like the one he knew in Kobe City to make his pants fit right in the crotch. He wishes he had never come to Tokyo after all. . . .

And the group of young women leaning against the train door in high-heeled boots and high-cut jeans, their luscious cheeks followed by the eyes of men riders and the other women in skirts and overcoats, looking so fresh and sculpted. . . . Who would dare assault them in a group like that? Tokyo is theirs. They primped in the windows and stared boldly around the train. One looked me up to down, and then down to up. On the up, our eyes met and locked; she turned suddenly and pulled on the sleeve of the closest woman. They talked about me, I could tell, because her friend stared at me in the window. They giggled and straightened their hair.

You needn't be so snobbish, ladies. I was very calm and not in the least offended by their whisperings. You are all quite fresh and attractive, I told them. By now the whole car was listening to me. You look just like the posters I see and the magazine covers, all of you, really. It seems more and more the young women I see could all be models. You, too! You are also the same women I see at night going home alone, each of you on separate trains with your eyes cast down at your hands or fixed on all the shoes or paging through some magazine watching shoes, all those men's shoes you see at night. There you are, you come into the train looking at all those shoes and smelling all the booze on the breaths, and who is it you choose to sit by? You search quickly for the nearest woman with an empty seat next to her, and you join her no matter who she is, just so long as she's female, and even if she's talking to herself it doesn't matter too much—all the better maybe, then no one will bother you at all because they're afraid of her! So many of you sit next to me, sleek hands and shiny nail polish turning pages of novels and magazines. And God knows I'd choose you too under the same circumstances.

But then again I might have been wrong about one of those two men talking with those coy office girls. Either I was wrong or his pants were way too tight. He was quite tall, for that matter. He was easy with both girls. Moreover, it was impossible to tell which one he liked. Both girls were being equally teased, only one of them able to come back with some teasing of her own. She directed a quick stream of benign insults at the other, shorter guy (the one with the pants that did fit), and he called her "Crazy Woman" in English, and then they all laughed. Ah, but she got him back! She tossed her hair now, pulled her hat over her nose, and began whispering secrets into her girlfriend's ear through a pile of curls. The two ladies giggled as the men pretended not to notice them. It was very light and happy.

The train filled up.

I smiled at the taller man with the tight pants. He looked at me at the same time my hood fell off onto my shoulders. My hair, glossy and full as my mother's when she was young, seemed to grow fuller before his eyes. I let go of the bag I held in front of my legs and carefully pulled my hood back on, tucking in the long ends. He turned back as the girls pulled him out the door. Their stop.

The man next to me let his hand drop to the space between us. I had seen that before. Next thing I knew, his hand would be reaching underneath me for a grab before he got out. I rose, swept past him with my bag into the next car. Through the heavy metal door: swing it back, smack it closed.

At the next stop I changed trains. Time for a change. The silver line called. Thousands of people streamed around me. It was another excellent day for riding. Shortly thereafter, in a rare and swift change of heart, I got out of the subway and switched to the green line, to check out the aboveground train.

18 | THE FIRST WAR BRIDE

I find myself collecting stories for you. . . . You will like this story that happened to me today. It has to do with America, and a certain stranger who found love there. Many people tell their stories to me, but I find it odd that the foreign ones seek me out. How can they know? If you decide you can like me, even a little, you can help me figure this phenomenon out. . . . That is what sisters are for, right?

She was standing with her back to me, a short, stocky woman with stringy black hair down to her shoulders and parted in the middle. She wore a white gauze mask over her mouth and was coughing. We were waiting for the train.

The others stood behind us and across on the other side where the door would open. I was thinking about all the face masks I had seen in the past few days, and wondered if I wasn't feeling a little scratchy in the throat myself. Also I was thinking about earthquakes. The weather was turning incredibly balmy—earthquake weather.

As the morning wore on, riders got on the train sweaty and holding their woolen overcoats on their arms, stuffing them in the upper racks; some even wore them though drops of sweat trailed down their foreheads and into their eyes. In the sun I let my hood drop off and bunch behind my shoulders.

Back on the silver line I had overheard a conversation between an older woman, sixtyish, I'd say, and her daughter, in her thirties, both of them distinguished-looking Shoppingbagwomen, talking about earthquakes: Of course it is only an old myth, but there is something fearful about this change in weather . . . they say the Great Kanto Quake of 1923 occurred just after such an unusual turn in the weather. And is that so, said the daughter, or is that a story you heard from Father? Of course it is so—I heard so from Mother, and she was there, you know, said the earth went straight up and down, like this! And the older woman lifted her palms up as if she were offering a present, then raised and lowered them sharply up and down, up and down. *Gatchan!* she said.

Other people were listening by then. Ooo—, the daughter shuddered. And then she said, Wow, it's scary, isn't it? And they fell silent. But the two Hitachi workmen who had stopped their talk about a colleague to listen to the two women began to discuss in a low tone the holocaust they feared when the gas lines blew up, and whether or not the building they worked in would be knocked down or burned or what. And then they laughed together; one patted the other on the shoulder as they made their way out of the train.

I was thinking about that, and rather wondering if we weren't going to have a tremor, when the woman in front of me turned around and looked straight into my face. She had warm brown eyes and appeared old-fashioned or Korean or American Indian, or something, out of place on this bustling platform with that hair hanging and parted so girlishly, her dark face worn and lined. She looked like an old doll I used to have, an antique given to me by my maternal grandmother from the country. Surely she was smiling at me under that mask! I couldn't tell, but I smiled back. She began to say something, but it started a fit of coughing and she turned around to face the train, which was by now pulling up to the platform.

When the doors opened, we found two seats next to each other in the center of the car. She pulled up her mask and began telling her story in a hoarse, high voice. She took care to cover her mouth partially with a handkerchief while talking.

"I work Red Cross Hospital," she spoke in broken English. Then she pointed to me. "You know Red Cross Hospital? Other side of station."

Was she talking to me? I waited. She waited.

I cleared my throat. "Ah, yes. I know. Across from Mitsubishi, isn't it? I used to get a good shoeshine out there in front of the building."

She nodded. "I work there. Three times week." She made a face. "Long way, you know. I live Yokosuka."

"Oh yes. That's a long trip for you."

"Long trip, yes." She was quiet. Then, "You speak Japanese?"

"Yes."

"Oh."

The commuters crowded in together as the doors opened. The warning bell sounded for the doors to close. It jangled away, only a meter above our heads. And when the bell finally stopped ringing, she spoke again.

"I was First War Bride." She smiled broadly, her voice filled with pride and emotion. "World War Two." She nodded emphatically. Her eyes twinkled. "First War Bride. Married to big American man. Irish. Ooh, he was big man. Flyer. Red hair. Six foot five about. Died plane crash."

She smiled fondly. "Kids—all the kids—red hair, too. Big. My son"—she lifted her arm straight up and indicated three heads above her own—"really big boy. Speak English only." She began coughing into the handkerchief. I felt sorry that she was so sick and losing her voice, but I was very curious to hear her story. I watched the feet of other riders for a while until the coughing pitched to a peak, then came to a gentle clearing.

"First War Bride? That's really something. How did you meet your husband?"

"I am born China. Father in Manchuria long time. So I born Chinese, but parents Japanese. Seven years I live China, then go back Japan. Many Japanese go back. After war I need job. Go to

American base to nice job; nice girl, sell candy in PX, meet nice man. Jimmy. He calls Chris to me. Chris, my name." She pointed to herself, and smiled.

"We got marry. Go back to U.S., have house Massachusetts. His mother think Chris no good, but give house anyway." She shook her head, and peering directly into my eyes, continued, "Big house. She no like Japanese wife. Never come to Massachusetts house. Not one time. Kids they go Boston, see Grandma. I"—she said, pointing to herself,—"I not go. She no come to my door, I no go there. No way." And she smoothed the sleeve of her Navy jacket. Then she laughed.

"Anyway, she sure like kids. All red hair." She began digging in her big brown bag.

"And your husband?"

A wallet produced! And photographs of three tall children with brownish-red hair, two boys and a girl. The two boys are standing behind their sister, who sits in a white lawn chair. The boys wear suit coats and have their hair slicked back, though one of them—the one with the easy smile—has an unruly cowlick; the other, with his shy smile, reminds me of an American actor whose name I have forgotten. The girl wears a sundress. Opposite that picture was a portrait, probably taken in high school, of the daughter, who has a sweet face and a slim gap between her front teeth. She looks directly into the camera, eyes deep brown and an air of innocence about her.

"My daughter," the First War Bride said.

"Where is she now?"

"U.S. She goes college. California. Stanford. You know?"

"Oh yes. Stanford's a good school, I heard."

"Good school? Hmm." She barely seemed to hear me. Flipping to the front of the wallet, she stopped at a photograph yellowed and creased, a full-length picture of a tall man wearing a pilot's uniform and a short Japanese woman in Western dress standing next to him, a broad smile on her face. Her hair is shoulder-length and curly, with curly bangs. The eyes are unmistakable—warm, deep brown, laughing. He looks boyish and soldierly. His arm is around her.

She flipped to another picture. It was a faded picture, in color, of a man with light brown-red hair and blue eyes. He wears a pilot's uniform with modest decoration. It is a studio portrait with a simple white background. And opposite that picture was a big, rambling, Victorian-style house surrounded by a huge lawn and maple trees.

We viewed it silently. She started to cough again and folded the wallet back up into her bag.

"You know Massachusetts?" she asked finally. Her voice was high and far away, becoming more strained with each word.

"I've never been there myself," I said, "though I'd like to, I guess."

Chris went on, "I been San Francisco, too. My son—now in California. U.S. Navy. Near San Francisco, I think. He no speak Japanese." She shook her head. "You speak Japanese?"

"Yes, I do. I grew up here. How did you know I speak English?"

She gave me a knowing look. "I know. You *gaijin*. You foreigner like me. I feel so."

She seemed to be waiting. It was my turn, I guessed. I spoke in English. "My father was Nisei from California. He came to study, work, and find a bride. He thought he wanted to live in what he felt would be his true home—here, in Japan. Sorry to say, he hated Japan. He spoke Japanese but he refused to speak anything except English to me and my mother. He sent me to an American school and told me about the cities he'd been to, and Hollywood, and the open stretches of land in America. He missed America."

"He go back, eh?" The First War Bride nodded.

"He was very unhappy. Very bitter," I went on. I could see him sitting very still, rice bowl and soup bowl in front of him, late at night, just sitting there, not eating. I was supposed to be in bed. Mama sat watching him, her legs folded underneath her. He began to complain about the company. He said he might as well be an untouchable from some *buraku* for all the respect he got. Then he would tell my mother, if they ever made fun of me in school, he'd go down there himself and let those nuns know how American his daughter was!

"So, eventually, there was trouble at his company, and then there was trouble at home. He just got quieter and quieter. My mother used to tease him, called him the Quiet Man—you know, like John Wayne, and . . . well, he just couldn't cut it, I guess. It's really kind of a long story. Mama told me later to watch out when a man got quiet. Like something bad would happen if a man got quiet."

Chris nodded, like she was saying, Go on, tell it all, tell it.

I said, "One day—I was eight—he just left. He went back to California. He cried because he couldn't take me. At least that's what my mother says. Every spring of the new school year, my mother—who spoke practically no English, you know—would sit me down in the parlor to tell me that my father had sent money for me to continue at the American school. Actually, I don't remember him too well anymore."

Chris didn't change her expression once as I told my story, but stared ahead at some point across the aisle. When I had finished, she said, "America is good place. Some people—mother-in-law, town people—not like Japanese so much. Think Japanese no good. Only some people."

She leaned forward, whispering in a coarse, tiny voice. "Many people—good heart. *Koko ga*"—she held her hand to her heart, patted it up and down—"here, is good." And she nodded several times, settling back in her seat. The train rattled on.

"My husband die plane crash. Many people come my door. Mother-in-law not come. Brother come. Brother—he hold my head—I cry. Many times cry. Many times, brother, he hold my head. We cry. We fall in love, got marry."

A gust of balmy air rushed in from the window opposite us.

"You married his brother?" I asked, not sure I heard her correctly.

She nodded. Suddenly I wanted to see the pictures again, but it was too late.

"He die Vietnam. He pilot, too. U.S. Air Force." Her eyes clouded. "He join Air Force like brother did too. Shot down. Vietnam. Over more ten years now."

My head throbbed. It didn't hurt exactly. It was just throbbing, like all the blood had decided it needed to show up at once to help me process this, this life of the First War Bride. God! If she would just back up a bit. But it was too late. She whispered on.

"Mother-in-law, she pretty fancy. Love those kids. Anyway, mother-in-law getting old. Come to my door first time ever. Kids all grown up, college, Navy. She cries, Oh my, I'm so sorry. I'm so sorry. Long time she cries. Katie—my daughter—she cries. I'm okay. Two husband dead, but U.S. pay every month. Good money. Buy food PX. My son come soon Japan. No speak Japanese." She smiled. Then she reached into her bag and, before pulling her hand out, asked, "You like Chinese food?"

"I love it. Yes. Thank you."

She gave me a tinfoil packet of Chinese sweet potatoes covered with large black sesame seeds and golden honey-taffy sauce. I saved it for lunch.

She left without saying good-bye.

19 Captured at Last

There was a free seat next to some schoolgirls. And there was a newspaper in the rack above my head. Good fortune! I pulled it down to page through.

Race news. Football in America. The Japan Bowl. New Year's song contests coming soon. Singer commits suicide and everyone wants to know if note is left behind. Why? They cry. Sexy story with illustration of a small-headed woman with an enormous ass. Weather unexpectedly warm in Tokyo and vicinity. Future of Japanese baseball. Cyanide poisoning in Bunkyo ward subway. Stationwoman of unknown origin found dead. Police seeking subway rider with long brown coat, brown hood, seen giving brown package to victim near time of death.

An icy wind blew in my head.

Stationwoman of unknown origin found dead. Police seeking subway rider with long brown coat, brown hood. . . .

In a cold panic I left the aboveground train, headed swiftly toward the subway that would bring me home, to the end of the line. Get home. Get home. My mouth went completely dry, and I could barely breathe. Before getting on the subway, I found the ladies' bathroom, threw water into my mouth, and stuffed my hood inside the back of my coat. It made a fat pile like a hunchback on my shoulders.

I did not stay in one car, but walked from car to car whenever I felt someone looking directly at me. The metal doors grew heavier and heavier. My bag got crushed as I opened the last door in the last car, thudding shut behind me. I struggled to free the bag. Don't tear the bag.

When I got off, I could see Stationmaster Ogino-san surrounded by a circle of blue-uniformed officers. There was no going back: I could not leave without going past the group. And I could not go back on the train. Ogino had looked up and seen me. He pointed. My heart pounded, and I could not catch a full breath. *Wait, wait.* I heard. *Wait.* Was it I who said, Wait? Or was it them? Did we both say it?

Without a word I waited, submitted to the group of officers coming boldly toward me. The chief was easy to pick out—the others half-trotted behind him, stern-faced all. I was pleased to see a female officer in the little group. She pulled on gloves as she strode closer and closer. I held out my bag to her. My hands were grabbed and held from behind.

I was shaking and breathing shallowly, but I was not scared. For all of a sudden—the instant I saw the policewoman pull her white gloves on—I felt like we had all rehearsed this before, and I had waited a long time for this production. I felt certain that the policewoman must have felt the same way. She stared at me coldly. They hustled me into the stationmaster's own glassed-in office off the platform, and Ogino hastened to clear off his desk and stand outside, out of the way of the serious business ahead. He carried himself like a hero. He was a hero, a true hero.

20 | *The Dunes Book* and Other Effects

In my bag the police found all the evidence anyone could ever need to indict me: first my notebook with all the scribblings and loose sketches I have done—my stationwoman, my sleeping men, people on the train. The name of my apartment house, Rose Maison. A brush. My money. My pen. Five officers squeezed into the room.

The one behind me tightened his grip on my wrists as the sketches came out. Though aware that I was shivering with cold, I was strangely calm.

It was as though I was watching a crime show that I had seen several times before on TV. The woman officer—a crime technician—pulled out a large crushed mass of aluminum foil with a long tonglike device. . . . *And now the tongs will find the potatoes Chris gave you for lunch.*

"There's a couple more things in there, chief," the policewoman called out. "A padded envelope with something in it. And a letter."

"Good. Let's see the envelope first."

"Careful," cautioned the guard posted at the door. "It might be coated with something."

"Don't worry. I've got it," said the operator of the tongs.

"What's your name?" the chief asked crudely.

I found myself whispering, "Rider. I am a Rider."

Do not say Mai. No matter what. I could not bear to say my formal name, for the shame it would bring on my mother.

The chief swore under his breath.

Out of the bag came more evidence. It was a padded postal envelope containing a small notebook, with a single sheet of paper folded inside. The envelope itself was addressed to Mai Asahikawa, Rose Maison Apaato, 3-14-20 Shimada-ku, Tokyo. In the return column was an address outside Osaka.

"Ho! Rider! Is this your name?"

"My name is Rider."

The chief swore again.

Mama's face floated before my eyes. *Doshitano, Mai-chan?* I heard her asking sweetly. (What's up, Mai dear?)

No, my name is Rider. For now. I shook my head from side to side. Soon they will discover all.

There was a letter inside the padded envelope.

"Read the letter. Out loud, so everybody can hear it," I heard myself whisper.

"Yo! Rider of the trains! Do you wish to make a statement?" barked the chief in my face.

I kept on shaking my head. From now on, nothing but silence.

"You'd better believe we'll look at everything here! Takada, you read it. Maybe we can get a statement out of Rider." His lips curled back off of large, gleaming gold teeth as he said the word "Rider."

"*Hai!* I understand." Takada-san snapped to attention, and began reading the letter.

Passengers strayed toward the scene in the glassed-in kiosk off the platform, pressing closer to find out what was going on.

"Wait a minute," growled the chief. Turning to his man guarding the door, he shot off a new order, "Keep those rubberneckers outta here! Call extra units if you have to!"

"*Hai!*" The guard let himself out, posting himself outside. He shut the door and began giving important-sounding warnings for the passersby to move on.

"Carry on," the chief nodded.

Takada read in a high, nasal whine:

Dear Mai,

I know you were a friend of my niece, Natsuko Ota. She spoke of you often, especially during college. You might have heard of me too, as Auntie Chako.

As you may know by now, Natsuko died with her children in her apartment last month. It is no secret that she took what she thought was an honorable way out of this life. The apartment was filled with gas at the time a neighbor boy came by for his English tutoring.

May the blessings of Buddha be upon her soul and the souls of Yuko and Sachiko.

As executrix of Natsuko's affairs, I am authorized to turn over to you her last journal. It was kept for some days by the police, but later released to the family. As it had your name on the first page, I felt it should go to you. There were several other books with your name in them, apparently books you shared with Natsuko. Unfortunately, these were severely mildewed and we ended up throwing them out. I take it they were unable to afford keeping their air conditioner on during the past summer, and I apologize on her behalf.

Our hearts share the same sorrow. Please, when you can, burn incense for our child, Natsuko, and her babies, as well as for Tomio, and for all the family. We are grateful to you for the many kindnesses you gave her in her life.

Sachiko Ueda

No one spoke at first.

"Sir, do you suppose this is related—" began Takada in a quiet tone.

"*Kora!* (Hey!) Prop up that booklet on this desk," interrupted the chief. "I'll read through this myself. I think I heard about this case in headquarters. Of course, these things are happening more and more, but I think I remember this one. About a year or so ago. Despondent housewife and all that."

The technician's tongs turned each page of the little notebook for the chief, who read silently, nodding when he'd completed each page. On the cover, written in Mai's own hand, it said, *The Dunes Book.* A magazine cut of an Egyptian pyramid, with sand dunes in the distance, had been pasted on.

On the inside cover was inscribed: "To Natsuko, love Mai."

The facing page showed a retitling by Natsuko. It read: "The Entombment of the Queen of All Reveries, by Herself."

As the chief turned the pages I was remembering the words, reliving her self-torment and final, determined despair—as if I and Natsuko were the same person, and had always been, something like the way funny and sad are both parts in the same personality.

I saw the tears falling, even before I knew I was crying. They splashed onto a filthy brown coat, covered with stains from noodles and cigarette ash. The tears seemed to be spilling out from all over and I felt the wet gush of mucus stream out my nose. As I turned to wipe my face against my coat sleeve, a sharp, searing knife of pain burned and shot all the way up my arms as the officer holding me twisted and dug deep into sensitive pressure points in my hands.

I heard myself cry out, *"Itai! Itai!"* (It hurts!)

"Oh, the Rider speaks!" jeered the chief. "Disgusting animal." He hawked and spit on the concrete.

Through the wall of water in my eyes, I could make out much of the journal as the technician propped it high for the chief to read. It has been written entirely in Japanese, in Natsuko's delicate, rolling hand:

> Sent Tomio off to work at six, with rice and miso in his belly. As usual he did not speak to me. He has not spoken to me for 101 days now. I am tired of begging him. Instead, I have grown accustomed to the silence. And when he answers the phone, I realize I am happier not hearing his voice. He speaks sweetly to the outside world, but wreaks his hatred on me.

I tried not feeding him, to get him to talk. But he simply kept more money on payday and ate outside. It was three weeks till he gave me enough money for decent groceries that time. I don't care about myself, but the children need more than broth and rice. . . .

He sleeps in the bedroom. I sleep with the girls, or out on the tatami next to the TV.

Today I got the letter from the lawyer of Nobu's mother and father. Well, Nobu warned me about the possibility that his mother might try to gain custody of Sachi, but still it was a big shock. It says there is a copy being sent to Tomio's office, to make sure he sees it. I feel certain he has not received it yet, or it would show in his face. Probably he'll get it today. . . .

The old biddy does not trust me at all, and she is very smart. I suppose she should not trust me. Anyway, how can she believe that taking a baby away from her natural mother would be a good thing? If they truly cared about their granddaughter, they would send me money to make ends meet better. . . . It is too late to make my appeal, and I have no money for lawyer's fees. . . .

When Tomio comes home . . . who knows what he'll do? Could it be any worse than it already is? I don't think I'm afraid. . . . At least now I'm glad that I told him the truth about everything, now that this thing has come up about Sachi. He would have found out anyway, it seems. . . .

But I can't help wondering what he will do now. He is the type that does *"Edo no kataki wo Nagasaki de utsu."* . . .

The chief paused. He looks up for a minute at the number-two man, Takada.

"This *'Edo no kataki wo Nagasaki de utsu.'* Know what that means, Takada?"

"Ah, it's hard to put in words, sir. To get revenge in Nagasaki for something that was done to you in Edo, or rather, Tokyo?"

"So. Young people don't know the old proverbs, it seems. It means when someone has done you wrong, you don't avenge your wrong directly, but you take it out on people in another place, in other ways."

"I don't get it, sir."

"Well, let's say your wife wants a mink coat, Takada. And you won't buy her one. So she turns around and feeds you brown rice for dinner, tells you it's good for your health, and she's not going to cook white rice anymore."

"But I hate brown rice," whined Takada.

"That's the point." The chief turned back to the journal. "Well, I don't know if this has any bearing, but we shouldn't ignore the possibility of foul play here too," he grunted under his breath. The stationmaster showed up with a subordinate, bearing cups of tea.

My chest ached and ached, and my head was filled and pounding. Tears streamed out, making their way off the coat, dropping to the floor.

Yuko came home crying from kindergarten again. The teachers scolded her. They told her that riceballs alone are not enough for lunch.

How can people be like that? Can't they stretch their brains to think that maybe I don't have meat this month? Instead, they scold her, as if it is her fault. I can't stand myself for the guilt. It's too much. . . .

"Perhaps if we put a sardine in your lunch box tomorrow," I said to Yuko, but that made her cry harder. The child really doesn't like sardines. "Or half an egg, how about that, sweetie?" I said. She quieted down then. I just can't stand to hear her cry. It feels like I spend most of my time trying to think up things to keep them from crying. . . .

The trouble is, it's the last egg I will have, unless I

barter with Mrs. Sano down the hall. She gives me eggs sometimes and even bread if I tutor her son, Jun. He's forever needing help with his English grammar. It's lucky I remember any grammar at all. Seems like I have forgotten so many words, so many poems, words to songs . . . so much lost. But if I were a real tutor I would make real money. I think Mrs. Sano is taking advantage of me. I know she is. And I don't know how to get out of it. . . .

"Is this some kind of bad poetry?" I ask of my day. Mai used to say that whenever anything went wrong.

God, if you are listening in there, or wherever, can you tell me why it is such a struggle day after day? Haven't I been punished enough? Now I must fight for my baby? All that I have left. Are you kidding?

. . . Baby's up. . . .

Yuko wanted to play out in the courtyard with her friends, so I changed Sachi, and got her a bottle. She doesn't want my breast anymore. I suppose it's just as well, only it was cheaper before. . . .

We all went down the escalator to the ground floor. As usual, the other moms nodded and smiled at me. I said hi to everybody. They wanted to talk about teeth, which was fine with me. "Is it a new one coming in?" "Well, I don't see it yet, but it seems like it might be. She had a fever last night and she's a little warm today." That kind of thing. Everyone wants to hold Sachiko. She's such a lovely baby, she smiles and laughs at everybody, even with a fever. . . .

Then everybody began to talk about Golden Week. Where their husbands are taking the family over the holiday, and getting train tickets and all that kind of thing. I started feeling really depressed, and so sorry for myself, and I felt like I wanted to scream at them. I feel so hateful it scares me. May seems a thousand years away. . . .

I tried to stay there on the playground—forced myself into ten minutes more, for Yuko's sake. Then suddenly she ran screaming after Jiro-kun, who had just taken away the ball she'd been playing with. At first I did nothing. I thought they might work it out. But then the mothers frowned, sort of, in my direction, so I ran out there to get Yuko.

"That's Jiro's ball, sweetie. It's not yours, Yuko-chan. Come inside with me now. Come."

But she twisted away from me and ran after Jiro, who was taunting her by then. Secretly I was thinking, "Good for you!" She's such a willful little kid. But now everybody was really looking, and there I was again, my mind scrambling to end this scene, the 857,000th scene like it. All of the other children come downstairs equipped with toys. Baseball bats and wagons and yo-yos and brand-new balls, and so much.

Yuko is afraid of losing any of her own, so she refuses to take them downstairs. She hasn't gotten any new ones since New Year's anyway. When we first started living here, I used to want toys for her. But now I think of all the junk there is everywhere, and I don't care if we have toys or not. But Yuko cares. . . .

Well, finally I just called to her, "The baby's wet, we've got to go!" and I left without her. Of course she was clinging to my leg by the time we reached the elevator doors. And sobbing all the way. Great. I wanted to say, "How about we read a book?" But I just couldn't. My head was pounding on all four corners, like a demolition crew or something.

All I wanted to do then was lay the baby to rest and put the TV on to get Yuko to stop crying. At least the TV still works.

It's the gas company that's not going to like us now. But I just can't pay the whole bill.

To make matters worse, Sachi's got this rash, poor thing. Her little bottom's so red and raw it's stained the diapers pink with blood. God. She cried at me when I changed her, like she was saying, Mama, can't you do something to make it feel better? That's when I broke down and cried. . . .

It's a good thing to have a journal. Even though Mai doesn't talk to me, I feel like I am doing the only thing I can by her, by writing in it. I know I put it off this long because I have nothing but my daily hassles to write about. Well, that too will change. I have decided what to do. I am going to ask Mrs. Sano for some eggs, feed us omelets, and rice. . . . Then I'll be sure Jun knows he's to come in at 8:30 sharp, as usual; the girls will be asleep by then.

"THE LAST BAD POEM"

Today is the last rash on a baby's bottom,
the last time a girl is scolded at school
for being hungry . . .
the last begging a poor poet
will do.
The only grace,
the only way,
if silence is punishment for my shame,
is to seek full measure, final rest
in the origin of silence itself.

REVERSAL OF THE ANCIENT PROVERB, NAGASAKI NO KATAKI WO EDO (TOKYO) DE UTSU

H*ai,* hold on to it," snapped the chief to the crime-lab techni-cian. She dropped *The Dunes Book* onto a sheet of plastic that had been spread out over the metal desk. It sat with all the other ef-fects, only a few feet in front of me. My bag was there, too. Only one thing left, I think.

"There's one more letter in the bag, sir," said Takada.

"Show me," the chief answered. "And get the Rider some tis-sues—that is, if It knows how to use them." The man at my back released my hands. A large pile of tissues was thrust into my lap. My hands were sore and trembling. I told them to be still; yet they trembled on.

The technician held her tongs in the bag, revealing a long let-ter, which she suspended in midair toward the chief. It has for-eign stamps and is marked AIRMAIL.

Yet another train pulled out of the station. In the distance, a low rumble sounded, like thunder from an approaching storm. The chief reached for the letter. The technician leaned forward across my face; then, suddenly, she pitched straight at my heart, tongs and all. As she fell toward me, an enormous explosion shook the station. *Ga-boom!* Glass burst and splintered.

Lurching forward out of my chair, I heard the man behind me scream, and I knew the glass must have shattered over his back: He had been standing with his back directly against the kiosk window. I pitched forward to land on the floor, underneath the heavy table, falling alongside the lab technician, whose arm was pinned under my chest. The top part of her body appeared to be outside the table, where flying objects came whizzing through the air, weapons all. With her free hand, she was trying desperately to cover her head. I felt a sharp pain pierce my chest, and I knew it had to be a shard of glass. I tried to rise, but there was nothing to hold on to. I was free-falling, and the ground was not there for me to lie on, only my pain and the sounds of crashing and breaking and groaning all around.

The Dunes Book slid onto the floor, within inches of my chin, along with everything else that had been on the desk. A telephone came flying next, hitting the technician square on the back of the head. Her head thudded heavily into the concrete. The arm under me grew limp.

I'm dying, I thought. I'm dying. Either the station is blowing up or this is the biggest earthquake in the history of Tokyo. In desperation I struggled to get up on my knees, hearing voices screaming outside the kiosk. What were they screaming? I listened.

Jishin! Jishin!—Earthquake!

My God, it had to be. And the earth rose up as a second explosion roared through the station. *Ka-boom!* Up and down the earth jarred itself mightily. I felt myself falling, felt the table lift off the floor even as I fell. Alternately I floated and slammed into the floor. A rung from the desk caught me on the back of the head and everything went black for an instant. Then, coming to, I realized I had to do something to stabilize myself. The earthquake was not coming to an end. It seemed to have a job to perform, and it would take as much shifting and rocking as it needed to, for as many minutes as it needed to.

Grab the leg of the desk! That's all I could think of to do. I rolled sideways off the still policewoman: the pain in my chest had been caused by her tongs. I was not bleeding after all! Still, it hurt just to breathe. I wrenched the airmail letter from the tongs. My letter! And I curled around the thick leg of the desk, somehow stuffing the letter deep into my coat pocket. I could see *The Dunes Book* within inches of my hand now. The movement had shifted from up and down to a sideways rolling, and I chanced putting my hand out to grab the journal. Just then the earth rose once more, slamming my hand down onto the book.

I was free-falling; no ground held on to anything now. The desk was flying up again, and I went with it. We crashed heavily onto the ground again. But *The Dunes Book* was at last in my hands! Elated, I thrust it into my pocket.

Suddenly, everything was completely quiet. The thunder had stopped. Then the moaning began. I heard the wailing: the wave of screaming and crying of people outside the kiosk.

Got to get out of here. Got to get out of here. Out of here. Out of here. I was aware that I wanted to lie still, to wait until the earthquake was completely over and done with. But the voice in my head was insistent. Pick yourself up out of here.

Tentatively, I rose. Even if the main part of the quake was over, aftershocks were sure to follow. I crawled over the body of the policewoman, and was on my way out when I remembered my notebook—my notebook with all the sketches and the notes I'd written about riding. Crawling back, I scaled the heavy boot of a man, searching, sweeping my eyes over the floor to find the notebook. I found it surely and swiftly, as if I had been pulled to it by a silken thread.

Get out! Get out! Back again, over the mountainous boot of the man. I looked to see what was connected to the boot. It was the chief. He had been felled by Ogino's filing cabinet. I didn't look back again, but crawled out to the platform, even as the earth rocked from side to side.

Side to side is better than up and down. Go! I spurred myself on.

Only when I got out the door frame did I realize what had become of the kiosk. It was total wreckage, nothing more than a shell of where a structure had been. Glass was everywhere and people were moaning all around me. I knew I had to risk standing up, to avoid getting cut.

I recognized Takada, the only policeman to escape, as far as

I could tell. He sat on the edge of the platform in a daze, trying to get his walkie-talkie to operate. It was not working. He tapped it repeatedly.

So, it finally happened, I thought. The epicenter must have been directly under the city itself. Chances were, it was chaos up above. Even if the epicenter was beneath Tokyo Bay, it would have to have registered off the scale to produce this much wreckage in the subway.

I could see giant cracks in the cement all along the platform. Bags and briefcases and magazines lay scattered across the platform and on the tracks. Children were crying, and frantic mothers held tightly on to their children's arms to keep them from running away. Many panic-stricken passengers had jumped onto the tracks and were huddled there on the rails in small groups.

A small tremor shook the tunnel, and the screams started again.

"It's not over!" someone shouted.

"It's a train coming!" shouted another. "Get off the tracks!"

People down in the train trench tried desperately to stand, but the earthquake threw them off center, and they fell down again and again like drunken passengers getting off the last train of the evening.

There was no train coming, I knew. There would be no train for a long time. For many years there had been a strict edict: In the event of an earthquake, the subway always shuts down completely. I had been in trains before over the last year of riding, when small tremors shook Tokyo. The procedure was always the same: The trains stop, wait, and then go again only when the all-clear comes through.

"It's not a train!" I called out to them. "Just stay where you are!"

"It's not a train!" echoed a man. "The trains aren't running!"

Some appeared not to hear. They continued to struggle against the lack of gravity, falling over and over again heavily in the dark soot of the tunnel.

At last the quaking stopped. Takada was still tapping on his walkie-talkie. He seemed to be talking into it as well, as though his wishing could make it work.

A group of twenty or so people headed for the stairs. I followed them. What of Rose Maison? What has happened to Emiko? I wanted desperately to find Emiko. But the people up ahead were stopping. Why weren't they making their way to the top?

Wailing started from the old woman in front and spread through the rest. Her kimono was askew and both feet were bleeding in her *zori*, bright red staining the white of her *tabi* socks. The ceiling way above the stairs had completely caved in. It was a solid block, impossible to get through.

"We're trapped!" called a college-age boy. "We're trapped!"

By now the group had swelled to over fifty people, as those from the trench hauled themselves up onto the platform, thinking they could escape by way of the stairs.

The old woman in front sat down on the bottom stair. She appeared to have moved from despair to prayer, singing out in a wavery low tone the chant of a Buddhist sect, *"Namyō hōren gēkyō. Namyō hōren gēkyō."* Over and over she changed, her eyes shut, body rocking. Her feet continued to bleed.

"You!" I said to the college boy. "Shut up!"

He looked at me angrily.

"Get your friend there to help fix up this woman's feet. At the least, prepare her a place to lie back and get her feet up, to get the pressure off!"

The college boy looked at the old woman for the first time. He seemed to snap to. His friend and others joined him, including a young woman who soothingly said, "Grandmother, let us lie you back and take off your *tabi,* to see what we can do." Gently, steadily, she talked the woman through the first aid.

I picked my way across the platform to the other end, hoping that the stairs at the opposite end were free. That was when I saw Ogino. He and several others had obviously been trying to exit from the escalator at that end. But an enormous metal bar had crashed down from the structure directly above the escalator, making a perfect lengthwise hit into the escalator itself. I guessed that as many as forty people could be under that one beam. I shuddered. There was moaning from the ruin, but I knew I could do nothing until rescue crews arrived. Still, even if they got here within the hour, these people would likely be dead. The air stank of body fluids and death.

The stairs had lifted upward to hit the ceiling, blocking any exit. So that's why they used the escalator, I thought.

Ogino was near the bottom of the escalator. Ever the hero, I thought, he probably hustled everyone up ahead of himself. Women and children, and male passengers first. The station was, after all, in his charge. I knelt near him.

"Shikkari shite," I whispered. "Hang in there." I have no idea if he heard me. For all I knew, he might have been dead.

I realized with a shock that we were trapped. This station and probably dozens of others were going to be like this for a long time. It could be days before we got out. . . .

I could see people from the group at the other end coming toward me. I headed back.

"No use in trying that," I said to them. Disheveled and panicky, the look in their eyes reminded me of the stray dogs I'd seen trotting sideways near the trash bins.

"I'm going there anyway," said one. He carried his left arm with his right arm, sling-style.

"Go if you like. But there's danger in wasting your energy," I said. "How long do you think we can carry on this way, with limited oxygen? The stairs are completely blocked off. And it's entirely possible that there are trains blocking the tunnels, which would be our only access to air."

"What she's saying makes sense," said a middle-aged salaryman to the man with the broken arm. "We'd better just sit tight and wait for rescuers to come."

From my vantage point I could see the rest of the group waiting in the distance. Obviously they had delegated this group to come after me and check out other escape routes. The old lady was still being tended, and two or three people were stretched out with others bent over them. Probably more first aid, I thought. That was good.

"I say that's not the best plan."

"What do you suggest then, bag lady?" said a third man. He was dressed all in black leather and looked to be in his thirties.

"My name is Mai," I said. "And I know these subways better than any of you."

"Ummm. She probably does," said the salaryman. I was beginning to like him. In some way he reminded me of Fukuzawa-san, my old boss from the trading company. Something in his manner. Something in the way he said, "Ummm."

"If we stay here much longer, we might as well die like the rest of them," I said. "It might be days before we're rescued. Who knows what it's like aboveground? If it's like this here, imagine the fires up there. Think about the debris in the streets. It could take days for them just to get the necessary equipment to this site. There's some food from the food kiosk over there, but it's just candy and something to drink, and not much at that. We'll run out of food. We may run out of air. And this auxiliary electric system that's running here now might be knocked out by another quake or a tremor."

Funny, until I said it out loud, I was not aware myself that the auxiliary power was what gave us enough light to see each other's faces. Ogino must have turned it on, I thought.

"Brilliant," said the man with the arm sarcastically. "We can all guess that much. So what do you propose we do?"

I had a bold plan. It was thinking about Fukuzawa-san that inspired the idea. It was just an idea, but it was our only hope.

Two more tremors struck. Light ones. Short ones. About twenty seconds each, back to back. Once again people were screaming; only this time there wasn't as much running. They hit the ground, holding on to the rocking earth. Probably 2's on the scale, someone said.

"In key stations along the subway line there are Lost and Found rooms," I explained once the tremor subsided. "This, unfortunately, happens to be a station without one. When people lose something here, they have to go to Mito—the next stop—to check out the storage facility there. Though this is the end of the line, they didn't place one in this station because it's not popular as a tourist attraction like Mito is. Also, Mito has that college there, you know."

"I know, I teach there," said the man I had pegged as a salaryman. So, he wasn't in business after all.

"Great. We walk to a Lost and Found station so we can feel 'found.' Is that it?" The sarcasm poured like acid from a leatherman. Ignoring him, I turned to the teacher.

"The Lost and Found room is well insulated—almost like an air-raid shelter," I said. "There are tons of bags with all sorts of foods and clothing and everything imaginable. An employer of mine once told me about it. We could shelter there safely for days, if we have to, providing there's adequate oxygen in Mito Station. If you can convince the whole group to go, we can make it by walking along the tracks. That is, if the tunnel hasn't collapsed. I don't think it can be too far. You're a teacher, they'll listen to you."

"I say we make it a group decision," the man with the broken arm spoke up. He looked back toward the busy group of people at the other end of the platform. "There's strength in the group. I think we should decide here first. I, for one, am in favor of going off to get lost and found."

His attempt to be humorous was welcomed by the group. Terse laughter followed. It was a good sign, I thought.

We ended up agreeing that the teacher and I would both lead. I was to organize the women as a team, and he would organize the men.

Our plan met with no resistance from the others. They were getting restless, and going anywhere was better than staying on, feeling trapped. Different people "assigned" themselves to each other: the leathermen were physical crutches for the old woman with the bloody feet. The woman with the small boy gave her son over to a man who agreed to carry him on his back, while she joined with the efforts of three people trying to calm Takada, who had become semi-hysterical. They convinced him to leave the broken walkie-talkie behind, and told him they needed an officer to come along "for protection." At that, Takada's mind suddenly turned the corner. This was something he could understand. He was still dazed, and made no moves toward me, nor did he give any indication that he knew how he had gotten there. I took it as a sign of grace.

The least injured, strongest of us, took the lead, jumping down the concrete sides of the platform into the ditch below, and helping the others as they scaled down the sides. Time and again, three or four of us teamed together to ease the descent of those who were injured and bleeding. The whole operation took forty minutes: the professor took note of the time and passed the information on to us, as if it was his duty somehow. By the time our entire group had assembled on the tracks, many of the screams on the platform had subsided. Instead, we heard moaning, moaning. From the escalator where the beam had crushed so many, and from those left behind on the platform, people too injured to move or be carried.

"We shall return for you!" vowed a middle-aged woman to the platform. "We'll tell them you're here! It's a promise," she said aloud to nobody in particular. Her voice was cheerful and clear— like a cheerleader's. As I looked, though, I saw that her voice belied her true condition: her face was a coursing river of ashen tears, each crystalline drop from her eyes blackened instantly from the dirt of the platform and the voluminous soot that fell in sheets from the ceiling with each slight tremor.

"*Sa,*" said one man, "let's go already."

Never was I so glad to be stranded at one particular subway station. Had it been way out by Maruzen, far from Tokyo's center, I thought, we'd be doomed. The crews would have gone there last, after they'd dug into the Ginza and Tokyo Station and surrounding stops. Or if we had been just one more station on the other side of Mito, not only would it have been perilously far to walk but it was such a long leg (about two full minutes traveling at top speed) the chances were good that we'd have met up with a dead train in the tunnel. The train would be standing there, useless, and people would be screaming inside and smashing windows and trampling each other to get out into the tunnel. . . . Just like during a strike, when the trains got too crowded—only worse. The idea of our little platform group crushed by hysterical humans from a train group sent a shudder down my whole back.

It was in this manner that I occupied my mind during the long, grueling walk down a darkness that stretched on and on. A minute had no meaning, I thought. Minutes, seconds, hours— all meaningless. On and on we trudged, one foot ahead of the other, marking slow time under our breaths, *"Ichi–ni, ichi–ni"* (One–two, one–two). . . . You would think we were a school class hiking Mount Fuji on All-Sports Day. . . . A class of all ages and sizes, all bound together by the same rhythm from schooldays. Instead of hot sun and fresh breezes, though, all we had were dank smells, and the acrid scent of train-rail metal, mere meters away from our shuffling feet.

Ichi–ni, ichi–ni, keeping close to the wall of the tunnel; *ichi–ni, ichi–ni,* not daring to walk in the blackness in the center of the tracks, but staying to one side always, carefully, single-file. Before starting down the tunnel, I had ordered the group to keep one hand continuously nudging the back of the person directly ahead—not in order to keep the line moving as everyone does during rush hour, but so that we wouldn't lose each other, so that each would regularly encourage the next person to keep moving, to feel that the way is safe.

I did not know quite how I ended up in front. I think it was the teacher who suggested I might know the way . . . As if a station person would travel the tunnels! Ludicrous though it was, I accepted his invitation to lead. I thought about each station along this particular subway line—one by one by one. Imagined them in shambles . . .

And I saw in my mind's eye the twisted wreckage of trains above ground. The green line—surely that was derailed somewhere along the squarish loop it makes in the city's center. Perhaps it had fallen into Electricity Street, erupting in a burst of fire and sizzle. . . .

I stopped counting *ichi–ni* out loud, so labored was my breathing. My heart ached. I stumbled—often. How could it be that Mito was this far? By train, it takes just thirty-six seconds . . . Was I wrong? Had I taken a wrong turn in the utter darkness?

A woman screamed as the earth jolted suddenly again. "No! No!!" shouted Takada. "Get down! *Jishin da!*"

Everyone dropped to the ground; teeth were chattering down the invisible line of people behind me. Fear shot through the group like electricity down a wire. By the time I felt the quake's full impact, I had determined it was just a small tremor.

"There'll be more like that!" I called. "Just a tremor. Side to side. It's normal."

"Just a tremor!" echoed the young man in leather. "It's okay, we can keep going."

"*Ichi–ni, ichi–ni,*" chanted the old woman in a wavering voice; for countless minutes now she had been hobbling along with her bloodied feet, holding on to first one man, then switching off for help from another.

Children were crying, "I want to go home!"

"*Ichi–ni, ichi–ni,*" the professor's voice resounded over their cries. "Keep it going. Come on, everybody. Only a little bit to go—to Mito—to safety. Come along. It's quieted down now."

After the train of people lined up again, touching each other's backs from the end of the line to the front to signal readiness, I took a short breath and slowly began working my way down the tunnel once more.

By now, taking deep breaths killed me, so sharp was the pain around my middle. And so I kept this light, surface breathing going: in, out, in, out. And this time I closed my eyes. I felt my way along the right edge of the wall, feeling not with my hands but with the outer edge of my right leather boot: hit wall, scrape down, step down right, step left. Hit, scrape, right step—that's how I handled the count of *ichi;* then left foot, for the count of *ni.* And so it went. . . .

Soon, I tuned out the murmur of the people following. Forgot about the knuckles of the professor pushing against the small of my back. Didn't care that Takada was babbling like a small boy; and erased the memory of Ogino's earnest face as he lay dying. Instead, I saw the white-robed priests who used to arch their bows in competition at the temple: I could still see them waiting, waiting, waiting . . . for that right moment when, at once, the mind and hand and Providence move together and the bow snaps! And everyone looks to see where the arrow has landed. There is no applause; there are no wild movements from the admiring throng. Instead, people just watch, silently, not so much observing where the arrow goes but watching the priests as the priests wait, and watching the bow as the bow waits, and watching others in the crowd as the crowd waits. . . .

It was an image I used to conjure up at times when I could not fall asleep. A memory of a scene from my childhood days, from a vacation Mama, Daddy, and I took in the ancient capital of Kamakura. I was very little, but the scene still was real, and oddly comforting as always.

I was just replaying the pull of the arrows when someone shouted behind me, "See—up ahead! It's Mito! *It's Mito!"* I opened my eyes. The station sign was hanging securely in the distance.

Mito. Land of the Lost and Found.

22 | LOST AND FOUND

As it worked out, curiously enough, we did have need of Takada's help as an officer. For when we did finally all make it over to the platform's edge, and I led everyone to the Mito Lost and Found room—along with an additional fifty others who were trapped at the station—we found that its door was locked shut.

Triumphantly, Takada pulled out his special officer's set of keys, which the chief had given him for any emergency that might arise. Everyone cheered.

The "facilities" were everything Fukuzawa had marveled over—and more. In going through the bags and boxes, resourceful people even found large porcelain and metal pots to pee in. These they placed outside the large room in an area of the platform, to keep the air as clear as possible.

I learned much of this later, as I spent most of my waiting time asleep on a pile of clothing. I hid in a far corner of the room and pretended I was hibernating. I was completely and utterly exhausted, and the bruise on my chest was so severe that I could not turn in any direction without extreme pain. Someone laid a long, roomy, woolen coat over me at some point; when I woke up, I took it as another sign of grace. Removing my old brown coat with the brown hood, I found Natsuko's journal, my own journal, and the airmail letter, and placed them deep in the pockets of my new royal blue coat. I would leave the brown coat behind.

I knew the contents of the airmail letter by heart. Just feeling it in my hand, there in my pocket, helped me through. I had no sense of day or night, nor hours or minutes. Just a being there, a waiting. Not hungry, not anything. Just waiting. And fingering this letter, which said, in a determined, round hand:

December 5

Dear Mai,

How are you?

I guess it's a bit of a shock for you to receive a letter from me. I confess that I have been more than a little distant in recent years, and I don't know quite how to apologize for that. Maybe one day you will be able to forgive me.

Your mom has written me to say that she is worried about you since you got divorced, and since your friend died. I am so sorry. I know you have been through a lot. Aiko also told me that you have quit working and suggested that a trip to America might be a good idea.

You may not know this, but for years I asked your mom to send you over here for a visit, but she was too angry with me, I guess. She told me it was God's will that you stay in one place, and that you had often told her you never wanted to see me again.

I'm going to go ahead and assume that Aiko gave me your address in Tokyo so that I could contact you directly. This letter is to let you know that I have made all the necessary arrangements in hopes that you'll come soon. An American passport with visa at the American Embassy is being prepared for you. All you basically need to do is give them your photograph, sign some papers, and wait a few days till the paperwork is done.

I also arranged for air tickets for you—to be picked up either by you or your mother any time at the main Japan Air Lines office in Tokyo. (Don't worry, they're roundtrip.)

Please think it over. Your half sisters want to show you where they go to school, and they have lots of questions

*about Japan. Melanie is studying Japanese, in fact. Nora
wants to meet you, too, and she loves a good story. She's
crazy about photography, so if you have any slides to show,
please bring them. You're the best person I can think of to
tell them what modern-day Japan is all about. I heard that
I wouldn't recognize the place, it's changed so much over the
years.*

*If you can't come now, I'll be patient. But Mai, I'm over
sixty years old now, and age does funny things to a man. Instead of relaxing in the "wisdom of my old age," I only think
about the places and the times where I was not very wise. I
have an unbearable ache when I think of you. Try to make
room for me. Please.*

*The landscape in northeastern Utah is vast and beauti-
ful, with open skies, high peaks, and broad basins. As you
have probably already guessed, California just closed in on
me too much after a while. I need more air, more natural
drama in my vista. I suppose I would have moved here
sooner, but the memories of the camps from when I was a
young man—in the war years just before I met your
mother—kept me away from Utah. Since I retired, though,
it made sense to come back. I've decided to explore all of
Utah's treasures, from the deserts to the canyons and mountains.*

*This area has changed a lot, and it's still growing, but at
a pace I can feel good about. You'll see a lot of buildings and
highways around the airport that gets you into the city, but
once you're out of the city, the land just opens right out.*

Thinking of you fondly, as ever.

> *Love,*
> *Dad*

The rescue crews got through to the Mito Lost and Found in
three days. They would have been there sooner except they had

been working their way through a stalled train with passengers still inside—several hundred meters down on the other side of the station. Many were dead. When I heard about that later, I realized with a chill that I had heard that very train leave the station, mere minutes before the earthquake struck in full force.

23 | Journey Of the Pebble That Grew into a Rock

Kimi ga yo wa
chiyo ni yachiyo ni
sazare ishi no
iwao to narite
koke no musu made.

May thy glorious reign
Endure for ages, myriad ages
Till the tiny pebble
Grows into a mighty rock
Coated with beautiful moss.

My sisters, perhaps you have heard the haunting melody that is the Japanese national song. "Kimi ga yo" is a song I wish to teach you. Some people think it has a negative message, that it is about the emperor and the great world war, that it means Japan wants to spread its power over the earth. I have some of my own ideas about it, and a new way of singing it, a new way to think about it. . . .

Hey. I see your face. I know you."

I hear the voice through a dream, a dream in which I am walking along a shore. Gulls fly by, wings glistening white in the sun. They veer out to sea in a group. I swim after them, but then I hear someone calling, "Hey. I know you." I struggle to open my eyes, and look into the face of an old doll I once had: it was wooden, and the light wood had turned dark over the years from constant handling. This face was lined with creases etched by worry and pain, but it was so familiar. . . .

"Hey. You remember Chris?"

There was a woman patting my arms at the sides. I was lying down, and everything around me was white—white walls, white ceiling, white table. My arms were dressed in white, and I felt so light, like an empty bottle.

"You come Red Cross Hospital. I see you, remember from train, after big earthquake. You call Chris," said the short, brown woman patting my arms.

"There. See? I work Red Cross Hospital three times week. Work more days now, every day, all time. Check on you," she added.

I nodded. I tried to pull myself up to look around me.

"No, no. You only rest. Chris take care."

"Why am I here?" I asked.

"*Koko ga*"—she patted my chest lightly—"here is pain in ribs and lung. Blood is weak—no so many red blood—you need red blood. And you eat now. Drink. Get strong."

The pidgin English was comforting. It was nice having Chris there. I couldn't believe my good fortune. For the first day after waking up in the hospital, I did nothing but drift in and out of sleep. Scenes from the earthquake haunted my dreams: the kiosk that shattered, the steel beam on the escalator, the tunnel, the moaning. It was coming back to me, but in pieces. Somewhere in there I must have remembered my mother's telephone number and given it to Chris, for she contacted my mother, and told me she'd arranged for her to come and see me. There was a shortage of hospital beds, and I wanted to leave as soon as possible. But I was completely unable to get up.

"A-mee-nee-a," Chris explained.

Anemia? How could that be? I wondered.

"You not eat good. I know—I give potato 'cuz you no eat. I see dat on train," asserted Chris.

While staying in the hospital, I had to pee in a basin. Chris just laughed at me when I complained about it.

Then she told me something I didn't know. Now that I was

awake, Chris said, I should know that I had become something of a celebrity.

"What do you mean, now that I'm awake? How long was I asleep?"

"Oh, three, four days. No wake. I watch. Newsmen come, try to wake Mai."

"But—what do you mean about—" My heart seemed to be pounding out of my chest. My stomach churned.

It seemed that the teacher who had been in my rescue group had told reporters about "the Subway Woman" and our entire ordeal, and on the second day of my hospitalization, newspaper crews from both the *Asahi Morning News* and the *Nippon Times* sought me out to talk about the rescue. Drifting in and out of consciousness as I was, apparently, I did not have a lot to say. They seemed to like that, though.

This next part I learned later: Two days after those stories were printed, the police volunteered an interview based on reports from another person in the famous "Lost and Found Rescue"— a police officer named Takada. "An investigation is under way concerning the link between the Subway Woman and the random poisoning of station people," was how the TV news ran. I have my mother and Chris to thank for keeping that particular piece of news from me.

My ribs hurt like hell. But I was anxious to get out of there. Supposing someone found out about the kiosk incident? And the stationwoman? I knew I had to get out—soon. Escape with Mama to the countryside. Before the reporters came back.

The day I started walking on my own speed, without any of the nurses helping me, was the day Mama arrived to take me home. To my complete and utter surprise, she wore a navy blue pantsuit and had her hair swept up loosely in the back—quite unlike her usual style when wearing kimono.

I hastened toward the long locker where my royal blue coat was hanging, eager to leave. But Mama stopped me by grabbing my hand. She sat down on my bed and said, "Now quit jumping around. We'll be home soon enough. I missed you, Mai-chan. Give a hug." We embraced and cried silently for long minutes together. It was calling me "Mai-chan"—that childish, affectionate term—that broke my composure.

"Mama! If only you knew," I sobbed. "If only you knew what I've been through. I heard your voice in my head, calling to me, 'Mai-chan, Mai-chan'—and it helped me, Mama. It did."

"Mai-chan," she said, smoothing my hair. "Look here. I know more than you think, but you're going to have to help me put it all together. Because I'm very confused. Here," she said, extending an envelope addressed to Mrs. Mai Asahikawa. "Here."

Mama had brought with her a letter of apology from the head of the Tokyo Department of Criminal Investigation. It seemed the stationwoman who died in Bunkyo ward had been deceased several hours before I was spotted leaving food for her to eat. A man who placed cyanide in open soda bottles turned himself in after two more station people were found dead.

"I showed this letter to the newspeople, Mai-chan. I had to," explained Mama quietly. "They were saying such bad things about you, Mai. They came to my house. So I showed them this letter of apology. I had to. Forgive me, Mai. It's for the family, you understand."

"Oh, God, Mama."

"They're here now, Mai-chan. They followed me here—I couldn't stop them. Tokyo Terebi reporters." As if on cue, there was a commotion outside the room. Tokyo Television—come to meet me, Mai.

"*Konnichi-wa!*" (Good afternoon!) called out a cameraman from the hallway. "We're here to meet the Moses of the Lost and Found."

"Mai, I'm not sure I like them calling you Moses. I think these people have no respect for Christianity," Mama said under her breath. "Can't you get them to change that?"

"I think it's too late," I whispered back. A perky reporter with her hair in a bouncy pageboy was talking a mile a minute into a hand-held microphone. About a daring rescue, and a brave woman, and about being falsely accused of a horrible crime, and the letter of apology from the Tokyo police . . . I had said nothing, yet she was already wrapping up the story.

Bright lights shone hot all around the hospital bed, where they'd been set up on tall black poles. A cameraman and three or four assistants hovered over me and Mama, who remained seated on the bed.

"Careful," I whispered to Mama, wincing. Every time she shifted her weight, my chest hurt.

"Totemo itai desu ne? It must hurt very much, huh?" said the perky reporter sympathetically into her microphone. She came closer to us. "Is it five or six broken ribs?"

"Three," I replied.

"Mai-san, I want to thank you for this interview. But before I go on to interview other victims and heroes of the devastating earthquake, I like to ask people such as yourself if you have anyone special you are looking for since the disaster."

"What do you mean?" I asked.

"That is, if you still are wondering about the whereabouts of a relative or a friend—or a boyfriend or something." She smiled coyly. "You can describe that person now, and if he or she is watching the show, they can call in on our special number. . . ."

My mind raced. This was a chance, a real chance. Surely there was someone I could ask for. The crew waited.

"Yes," I said at last. "I would like to know if a certain little girl is all right."

"Very good," the reporter leaned into the camera. "We're about to help locate a very special little girl for Mai-san. Please listen carefully, and if you know anyone that fits this description, please dial our hotline number with any information you have. Go ahead, Mai-san."

"Her name is Emiko. She's about seven or eight. She lives near my old apartment house, Rose Maison in Shimada-ku. She lives alone with her mother."

"Excuse me, Mai, but do you know this little girl's last name, or is there anything that might help our viewing audience figure out which Emiko this is? There must be a hundred thousand Emikos out there."

"I'm sorry, I don't know her full name." I thought quickly. I couldn't say on the air that her mother was a hostess-san. That was out of the question.

"The Emiko I know has two carved Hokkaido bears," I blurted. "She found them outside the Rose Maison Apartments."

"Thank you very much, Mai. Emiko, if you're out there, get your mother to call our station, will you please, honey? This is Eiko Yoshiyuki with the latest post-earthquake update, for Tokyo Terebi News at six." The lights went off.

After the news crew packed up and left, Mama took me back to her house outside Tokyo. I did not worry about Emiko again. I knew I had been given one last grace by a reporter named Eiko Yoshiyuki, and I had to trust that. Besides, I had other business to take care of with Mama. New Year's was already upon us.

I told Mama I wanted to light incense on New Year's Eve, in the Buddhist tradition, and asked her to go to the local temple with me. I knew she disliked going since she was Christian, but I asked anyway. She agreed to go, on the condition that I would go to Catholic mass with her the next day.

On New Year's Eve, both of us dressed in kimono. Mine was an old one Mama had had from when she was in her early thirties. It had shades of green and orange and gold, with an *obi* belt that pictured waves of the ocean. Hers was an elegant deep purple. I could scarcely believe it, but Mama seemed to be wearing nothing but *obaasan* (grandmotherly) colors these days, colors like purple and navy, the subdued shades reserved for women over age fifty-five.

In my hand I carried a small box of green incense. We walked slowly, as my ribs were still mending, and close to midnight so I would not have to wait outside in the cold too long. It seemed like there were hundreds and hundreds of people there at the mountain temple.

"For a small temple there sure are a lot of people," I said to Mama.

"That's because this is one of those on the Buddha's pilgrimage tour, you know," said Mama. "It may be small, but it's considered good luck to hear the bell chime here." As she walked, she nodded and smiled and bowed at neighbors and acquaintances who recognized her.

"They're surprised I'm here," she said in my ear. "But they're too polite to say anything."

The air was crisp and cold. The sky was the clearest I could remember. People crowded twenty-deep in front of the incense trough, good-naturedly waiting their turn to light individual sticks of incense. The pungent smell reminded me of Aunt Kaoru.

When I said so, Mama nodded. "I was just thinking of her myself."

I guess it was because Aunt Kaoru was always the one to keep up the family's Buddhist altar at home. Tonight it would be laden with fresh mandarins and other fruit in season, and a bowl of *sekihan*—festive red rice—for the departed ancestors, plus other New Year foods. It came to me suddenly that she too was at a temple in her town right now, probably lighting incense with Uncle Taro and maybe my cousins as well. Perhaps that was why I thought of her now.

The closer I moved to the burning clouds of incense, the more I heard the heavy murmuring, the quiet crying, and the occasional wrenching sound as a gasping sob escaped uncontrollably from someone's throat—the raw noises of people mourning for loved ones lost, asking for their salvation in death.

Finally, it was our turn.

"Mama," I said, "you hold the matches." I commenced to burn stick after stick after stick, watching each slender green end burn, then blowing it out, releasing the smoke, then poking the stick into the sand along with all the others.

I did not cry, but instead tried to think of each face or each group of faces that I lit for. I knew that if I cried, I would not be able to see the faces clearly. "God, let me feel the grace inside," I whispered. I lit a stick for all those I could remember who died in the earthquake, for Ogino-san the stationmaster, for the persons trapped in the escalator, for the poor stationwoman; then for all of my dead relatives and ancestors; and finally for little Sachiko, her sister Yuko, and for Natsuko.

"I love you," I whispered. "May your souls find peace."

I took out one more.

"This last one's for me," I declared to Mama.

"It's not usually done," whispered Mama in my ear, looking around to see if anyone had heard.

"I know that. I'm not your usual person." I lit one last stick of incense.

We stayed to hear the ancient temple bell as it rang out one hundred and eight times. The chiming was to cleanse listeners of the one hundred and eight sins one can commit in any given year. I could feel the bell vibrate in my chest.

"Do you think there's only one hundred and eight sins?" I teased Mama. "What do the Catholics have to say about that?"

"They say I had better pray harder for my strange child," she said back.

We walked home in silence. *Zori* sandals do not make much noise. Only the leaves rustled, and we could hear low chatter and scattered laughter from the little clusters of people around us.

I looked up at the moon.

"Are we having soup with that gooey *o-mochi* in it tomorrow, Mama?"

"Of course, Mai. But after mass."

Tired from all the walking, I asked Mama to roll out my bedding for me, and I went straight to bed. I slept deeply, without dreaming, for the first time in several days.

As I promised, I joined Mama for early-morning mass. The church was in a small wooden building. On the right side, in an alcove away from the pews, were rows and rows of burning white candles. After leaving money in the box, we picked up a handful of votives.

No one needs to be the match holder in this ritual, I thought. You can light candles from an already lit one.

"Ready?" Mama whispered.

I lit candles for family first—for Mama, for Aunt Kaoru and her family, and Dad and his family in America. Then a candle each for Natsuko's Aunt Chako, Tomio, and Nobu. I also included my German friend Sabena, and Fukuzawa, and anyone else that came to mind. I just kept lighting them, one after another.

"Mai-chan. People are looking," said Mama in a low tone.

"Don't worry, I just need one more. Come on."

"I suppose I can guess that's for yourself?" Mama whispered.

I nodded, smiling.

It was a New Year's I will never forget. I was busy that whole week, but not with church or temple. That's not for me. From the fourth day after New Year's, the day when stores reopened, I was shopping with Mama, and I kept right on shopping for the next two weeks. I spent one day taking care of some business in Tokyo. And I was packing.

I was packing at the time when Mama walked into my room and said, "Take *o-mochi* with you, Mai. As a gift from me. He . . . he likes it."

"Are you serious? Won't it spoil?"

"Not a chance. It's sealed tight."

"Okay."

"You'll need some other little gifts to take along," Mama added. "How about lacquer bowls or something Japanesey like that? Or some silk things—scarves—and maybe a necktie."

"Fine."

"Well, which would be best? We have to decide."

"You decide, Mama."

"What are you daydreaming about, Mai?" Mama came and sat next to me.

"Emiko. I was just thinking how good it is to know she's alive." I was memorizing every word of a recent conversation, knowing I would always remember.

Emiko and her mother had called Mama's house on the third day of the New Year. I heard a woman's voice first on the other end.

"*Moshi-moshi*—Happy New Year. I'm sorry to disturb you and your family at the time of the holiday, but . . . I am calling to find a Mai Asahikawa who used to live in the Rose Maison Apartments in Tokyo. I'm Emiko's mother." The voice was tentative but pleasantly deep.

"This is Mai. How do you do? I am so glad you found me."

"How do you do? So it's really you. Thank you, thank you! We were so surprised to find little Emiko knows someone who has saved so many lives. Someone so famous that she is on the news. Emiko found your number here by calling the hotline set up by the news station. She did not waste any time calling it, but I'm afraid it took some convincing before I would believe she really knew you. I asked several of my friends about it before I decided we should call. Forgive me. I am indebted to you for being kind to my Emiko," she said.

"How is she? Is everything all right?" I asked.

"Allow me to put her on and speak for herself. And again, thank you."

"It was nothing. I did nothing. *Kochira koso*—It is I who should be thanking you," I said.

Then I heard the woman call in the background, "Emi-chan! Emi!"

The little girl's voice was trembling, but I recognized it right off. We talked for a short while, about things like school and the time Emiko saw me on TV, and I told her I had heard that Ueno

Zoo had been damaged, and did she know that the pandas had been moved to Nagoya for the time being? Yes, she said, just until the zoo could make them some new living quarters. It was good both pandas made it through the quake, we agreed. Then, at last, we said good-bye. So long.

Before I got off, her mother came on again. She inquired if I would be moving back to Tokyo.

I told her no, I didn't plan to return to Tokyo.

That I was going to America . . .

That I would be gone "for a month or two, maybe more . . ."

Author's Note

In recent legislation enacted by the Japanese Supreme Court, children born to Japanese mothers and foreign fathers now may claim their rights to Japanese citizenship. This story is set in the 1970s, however, when no such rights were recognized.

Rider is a work of fiction. Names, characters, places, and incidents either are the product of the author's imagination or are used fictitiously, and any resemblance to actual persons living or dead, events, or locales is entirely coincidental.